DOOR OF DEATH

Sullivan was trapped with the corpse of his friend in the hotel bathroom, and the killer outside.

Pressed against the wall, he saw a bullet hole appear in the door, and then another.

"Shit, you sonuvabitch!" Sullivan gasped, in his best imitation of a dying man. "You've shot off my goddamn balls!"

The door creaked open. A hand with a gun emerged.

Sullivan fired two shots in quick succession, and shot that hand right off at its wrist. The gun went flying, and the hand hung for a moment from shreds, swinging, spurting red.

Then Sullivan swung to face the door and deliver the final blow. Suddenly he saw a hand grenade flying at him through the doorway. . . .

Exciting Reading from SIGNET

THE PSYCHO SOLDIERS

THE SPECIALIST #4

JOHN CUTTER

A SIGNET BOOK

NEW AMERICAN LIBRARY

PUBLISHED BY
THE NEW AMERICAN LIBRARY
OF CANADA LIMITED

PUBLISHER'S NOTE

This novel is a work of fiction. Names, characters, places, and incidents either are the product of the author's imagination or are used fictitiously, and any resemblance to actual persons, living or dead, events, or locales is entirely coincidental.

NAL BOOKS ARE AVAILABLE AT QUANTITY DISCOUNTS
WHEN USED TO PROMOTE PRODUCTS OR SERVICES.
FOR INFORMATION PLEASE WRITE TO PREMIUM MARKETING DIVISION,
NEW AMERICAN LIBRARY, 1633 BROADWAY,
NEW YORK, NEW YORK 10019.

First Printing, August, 1984

2   3   4   5   6   7   8   9

 SIGNET TRADEMARK REG. U.S. PAT. OFF. AND FOREIGN COUNTRIES
REGISTERED TRADEMARK — MARCA REGISTRADA
HECHO EN WINNIPEG, CANADA

SIGNET, SIGNET CLASSIC, MENTOR, PLUME, MERIDIAN
and NAL BOOKS are published in Canada by The New American
Library of Canada, Limited, Scarborough, Ontario.

PRINTED IN CANADA
COVER PRINTED IN U.S.A.

To Bertram Wooster
and John Shirley

My two best friends

1

A Walk in the Park;
A Shot in the Dark

It was a cool night in mid-April on Central Park West, with the fireflies doing a luminous square dance in the grove of trees to Sullivan's right, and the soft breeze mingling the perfumes of daffodils with the monoxides of passing taxis.

That's what it was like the night the killing began.

It was about eleven-thirty that Tuesday in Manhattan when Sullivan realized he was being followed. In fact, the man had been following him for half an hour. Sullivan would have noticed it earlier if he hadn't been so deeply lost in thought. He'd been thinking about healing. He had to heal during the winter, both physically and emotionally—physically, because he'd taken a gunshot in the shin last fall, and emotionally, because he'd lost two close friends, Malta and Snag, in that same firefight. Very nearly the only friends he had. Jack Sullivan was not a man who made friends easily.

After the red-fingered work he'd done that fall on the Rogue River, he'd steered clear of mercenary employment.

But despite constantly working out, despite the target practice and karate bouts, Jack Sullivan was feeling restless. Was it because it was spring?

No. He knew better. No use kidding himself. It was because he *needed* the work—not financially. But deep in his gut, he needed to fight the enemy, and always would. Who was the enemy? The enemy took on many shapes, many hats, many uniforms. But behind all its guises—heroin pusher, terrorist, mobster, psycho killer—the enemy was simply human evil. The urge to crush and dominate, to vampirize, to enslave, to kill for gain—human selfishness at its purest. That was Sullivan's enemy. Whenever it made itself known, a victim was created, someone who needed avenging. And vengeance, righteous vengeance, was Sullivan's specialty.

Which is one reason other hired fighters around the world called him the Specialist.

Jack Sullivan, the Specialist, was strolling along the sidewalk under the trees of Central Park West when some instinct stirred him from his reverie and made him glance over his shoulder.

The little man following him was half a block back, but Sullivan recognized that broad-brimmed panama hat and the unseasonably heavy coat. He'd noticed the man earlier in a bar, and again on the street shortly after he'd left the bar. He hadn't had a look at his face.

Was the guy really tailing him? Easy enough to check out.

Sullivan looked around. To the left, across the street, stood a row of stately apartment buildings, each with its awning and suspicious doorman. To the right was an asphalt path through the wall bordering the park. Okay—he'd head into the park. If the guy followed him in *there*, this late, he was following seriously.

Sullivan swung right, and strode briskly up the asphalt path into a part of New York that even trios of cops are reluctant to penetrate at this time of night. The wooded section of Central Park.

He paused at the first bend and stood half-turned toward the street, lighting a cigarette as he pretended to study the golden moon poised above the elm branches overhanging the path. Out of the corner of his eye he saw the figure in the long coat and broad-brimmed hat turn onto the path and start up the slight slope.

Okay, Sullivan thought. If you want to play, we'll play.

He turned away and hurried around the bend in the path. Ten strides farther on he came to an island of light around a lamppost. The glass lamppost fixture was half smashed away, open like a seashell; moths ticked at the humming bulb. Below and to his left was a stand of large plastic garbage cans—one of them open and empty—and a concrete-backed park bench from which vandals had pried most of the seating boards. Sullivan ducked behind the bench, which was partly overgrown by ivy, and waited.

Moments later his tail came gumshoeing around the corner, bent a little at the waist as he took the slope, looking from side to side for the man he'd been following.

He paused under the lamp, and Sullivan heard him muttering, "Son of a bitch . . ."

Sullivan wore a Beretta Brigadier in his shoulder leather, under his light suit jacket; he even had a permit for it, which had required some string-pulling by friends in the FBI. On an ankle strap just under his trouser cuff was a tempered-steel stiletto. But Sullivan decided that neither weapon was called for just yet.

So the Specialist used the other two weapons he carried with him always: his bare hands.

He moved whisper-soft from behind the park bench, stepped up behind the smaller man pausing in confusion under the lamppost, and clamped one steel-banded hand over the man's mouth, the other twisting his right arm behind him. Sullivan chuckled as the smaller man shrieked into his palm and struggled. Then in two deft movements he lifted him up over the empty garbage can and jammed him down into it headfirst.

"Hey whaddufuck you ..." came echoingly from within the can as Sullivan shoved the little man's legs down into it and clapped the garbage-can lid onto the top, bottling him up like a frog in a jar.

Feeble bangings came from within the black plastic garbage can as Sullivan picked it up and, holding the lid shut, carried it off the path and up the hill.

He found an open place atop the small hill, flooded with moonlight and the glow from the streetside lamps, and dumped the garbage can so heavily onto the ground that the man inside yelped with the impact.

Sullivan drew the silvery Beretta and waited. The Beretta glinted with moonlight in his hand.

The little man backed out of the garbage can, cursing, and sat back on his haunches. He still wore the hat, which now was stained and badly rumpled, and its down-turned brim hid the upper half of his face.

"What did you have to do that for?" the man demanded, sounding outraged. "My suit! My coat! All slimed up, dammit!"

"If I decide that your seeming to follow me was a coincidence and you're innocent," Sullivan said slowly, "I'll apologize and pay for the suit. But you'd better talk fast. Because if I don't get *some* kind of good explanation, I'll put a bullet in you. I have too many enemies."

The smaller man reached up and whipped the hat off. "Dammit, Sullivan!"

Sullivan stared. The face was familiar ...

And then he remembered. "Knickian!" Knickian was an agent for the Defense Intelligence Agency—the Pentagon's espionage service.

In the course of his Mission of Vengeance on the Rogue River, Sullivan had come up against the DIA, which was mounting its own action against the terrorist-training camp there—an action Sullivan felt was too slow and ultimately doomed to failure. He'd had to put Knickian on ice for a while to keep him from interfering.

So Sullivan kept the gun leveled.

"Your people still mad at me, Knickian?" he asked the little Armenian. "You got the files I took from the Blue Man, right? I sent 'em express."

"We got 'em." He added grudgingly, "They were useful. Real useful. You're not on our shit list. Put away the piece, you big ape. Think you're pretty cute with your garbage cans. Twice my size, goddammit."

Sullivan grinned and holstered the gun.

He bent and helped Knickian to his feet, dusting him off with exaggerated sweeping gestures.

"Okay, okay," said Knickian, annoyed. He stepped back and looked Sullivan in the eyes. Knickian was a fox-faced man, with hard dark brown eyes and a hook nose. Sullivan, well over six feet, two hundred pounds of muscle, towered over Knickian. But the little man stared defiantly up at him and said, "No more kiddy games. I need your help."

"Yeah? And so you follow me down the street like a goddamn Mafia punk?"

Knickian looked sheepish. "I wasn't sure I had the right guy. You shaved off that beard you had last time I saw you. And I was having trouble getting a good look. I didn't want to just walk up and ask, because I thought you might bust me up for what happened last time we got in each other's way." He shrugged. "I thought if I could get a positive make on you and where you lived, I could set up a meeting where I'd have some backup in case you were sore."

Sullivan chuckled. "I thought you people were pissed-off at *me*." He pointed at Knickian's shoulder. "Anyway, no more recriminations. You've suffered enough: you've got moldy potato chips on your shoulder."

Ten minutes later they were on the path headed toward the street. They paused a moment beneath the lamp while Sullivan lit a Lucky Strike for each of them and passed one to Knickian. "What do you mean, you need my 'help'?" Sullivan asked. "You—or the DIA?"

"Both."

"I thought," Sullivan said dryly, "you were against the 'involvement of civilians in government business.' "

"Normally. But the agency is paralyzed. All the agencies are, in this case, because they're getting misinformation. The problem has to be solved by someone from the outside. Someone objective." He blew cigarette smoke at a moth fluttering near his face, and went on, "It's like this. A group of KGB-controlled terrorists kidnapped the president of a big electronics firm—one with a government contract—and most of his family. I think I know where they're being kept, but there's a mole in the agency who's using his influence to get me labeled a 'crank.' No one'll listen to me. He's got 'em thinking I'm crazy—and I can't prove he's a mole. The guy who tipped me committed suicide—or somebody made it look like suicide."

They were just turning off the path onto the sidewalk along Central Park West, and Sullivan found himself wondering if in fact Knickian *was* a crank. Knickian spoke with obsessive intensity, and his hands shook with suppressed anger. There were plenty of espionage agents who'd succumbed to paranoia, imagining "moles," KGB plants in their organizations, crawling out of the woodwork. It was just possible Knickian had gone off the deep end. After all, Sullivan had heard nothing about the kidnapping Knickian mentioned.

As he was thinking this, another part of his mind was registering the sound of an oncoming car on the almost deserted street behind them. There was something not quite right about the sound of that oncoming car. It had abruptly sped up, gunning its engine . . .

Sullivan glanced over his shoulder, and his eyes widened as he saw the dark blue sedan bearing down on them, jumping the curb to angle across the sidewalk—

The bastard was trying to run them down!

Sullivan shoved Knickian aside, pitching him head-long over the wall and into the park bushes. Sullivan leapt after him, and the car screeched by, sweeping over the spot where both men had stood a second before. The blue Buick failed to straighten out in time and skidded to gouge its right-front fender into the park wall. A tire blew with a *bang!*, and metal protested, deformed by the wall. The engine coughed and died, the car stopped, having gouged out a yard-wide chunk of brick.

Beretta in hand, Sullivan looked over the top of the wall—and ducked back down as a slug from a .45 automatic smacked into the brick just below his chin.

He'd had a glimpse of four men piling out of the car. All of them carrying automatics. Pale, grim-faced men.

Knickian, a snub-nosed .38 in hand, was moving in a crouch up the hillside, into the bushes. Sullivan followed.

They reached the bare hilltop—bare of foliage but studded with waist-high gray boulders—and turned to see two of the armed hardmen, both wearing dark three-piece suits, one with horn-rim glasses, coming at them not more than twenty feet away, guns roaring. Bullets whined off the boulders, and the shadowy earth of the park was lit by muzzle flashes.

Knickian and Sullivan each fired twice. Knickian's first shot missed but his second smashed his target's left knee into splinters, sending the man tumbling down the slope. Sullivan's shots took out both lenses of the other man's horn-rims; blood spurted through rings of smashed glass as the man screamed and toppled.

A third man leapt to the top of a knee-high boulder ten feet to Sullivan's right and, grinning, said, "Drop it."

He had a German accent. East German? Sullivan wondered.

"You forgot to notice something," Sullivan told the dark, toothily sneering stranger.

"What's that?" the man asked, frowning.

"When I turned to see you on that rock, I brought my gun with me."

He squeezed the trigger twice, and the Beretta sent two 9mm Parabellum tumblers into the hardman's chest, knocking him off the boulder before he could think to aim and fire.

There was a rustling in the bushes behind.

"Down!" Knickian yelled.

Sullivan threw himself down and rolled, as a gun roared in the bushes, and .45 slugs kicked up the dirt where he'd been standing.

Sullivan and Knickian came up firing, the slugs shredding the leaves of the bush—but the unseen gunman had already taken off. They could hear him plunging wildly down the hill, smashing through the shrubbery.

A groan drew their attention to the wounded man beyond the boulders.

They moved cautiously down the hillside, and found the man with the shattered knee trying to crawl off through the high grass. He had tied a tourniquet around the leg, but Knickian's slug had broken an artery and blood pumped the killer's life away despite his meager first aid.

The hardman rolled over onto his back—and in his hand was a U.S. Army hand grenade.

And he'd pulled the pin.

He held the grenade's lever down to keep it from exploding. When he relaxed his hand, it would go off in two or three seconds.

"Come and get me," he snarled.

"Toss that egg down the hill, man," Sullivan said. "And we'll all live. Surrender and we won't kill you. We only need a few questions answered—"

"Yes, I know how you would ask these questions. And I would not live two weeks after I answered them. So I will die now—without treason. I hope you choke on your own blood."

He let go the grenade's lever. Sullivan and Knickian leapt headfirst down the hill, shoulder-rolling.

The grenade blast mingled its roar with the scream of approaching sirens. The cops had finally decided to put in an appearance.

Bits of sod and twigs rained down after the explosion along with something ragged-wet that might have been human flesh. Shrapnel whizzing over their heads knocked out a streetlight on the corner.

Sullivan sat up in darkness. He called out tentatively, "Knickian . . . ?"

"Yeah. I'm here. I'm okay. Let's get outta here. I don't want to explain to the cops. They'll hold us pending investigation and the DIA will be called in, which will mean the agency's own personal KGB plant will smear me and probably try to make these bodies look like anything but what they are, and—"

"Okay, okay, I get the idea. Come on."

He led the way up to the hilltop. In the moonlight they paused to look at the body of the man Sullivan had shot off the boulder. Sullivan reached out and turned the man's lifeless face to catch the light.

"I *thought* he looked familiar," Sullivan murmured. "I remember this guy—from Saigon. About '71. He was a KGB man, one of their thugs. Looks like he didn't advance in the ranks much since then."

"Hey you!" A cop's voice, from a little below them. Sullivan glanced toward the sound of the voice. A flashlight beam fenced with tree limbs in the darkness, then swung toward them. "Stay where you are! Jeezis Chris', look at that, Dan! This one's blown in half!"

"Goddammit, Bernie, you gonna be sick now?" came the other cop's voice querulously.

Sullivan and Knickian slipped into the woods and loped off across the park.

The cops were reluctant to search the park thoroughly—it wasn't *safe* in there—so the two fugitives had no trouble escaping.

On the far side of the park they emerged at Fifth Avenue, dodged hastily across the street, and, guns tucked away, entered a bar.

They both needed a drink.

Set up in a wooden booth with a neat whiskey apiece, the two men looked warily at one another across the table. Then Knickian said, "Sullivan, you knew that guy was KGB. And they are trying to kill me. They must have followed me while I followed you. So they want me shut up in a bad way. So . . . you believe me now? You gonna help me?"

Sullivan knocked back half his Johnnie Walker's, sighed, and said, "Knickian, we got a lot to talk about. Mostly it's you who's gonna talk. You talk. I listen. Get started."

2

Flashback into Horror

"I guess you didn't see the afternoon papers,"
Knickian said, "if you don't know about the Bremmer
kidnapping. Carl Bremmer, and his daughter. The
kidnappers killed Bremmer's wife, a son, and a niece,
a girl of thirteen. All three of the victims—the boy
too—were raped by the kidnappers before they were
butchered. And I mean butchered."

Sullivan shook his head. "That sounds like psycho
killers. Not a political grab. Not even the IRA would—"

"They *are* psycho killers," Knickian interrupted.
"They're set up to *look* like a far-left radical organization called the New Minds Liberation Army. I've identified their leader as one John Swenson, a maniac who
makes Charles Manson look like Mahatma Gandhi.
He doesn't really give a damn about politics, left or
right—none of the NMLA do. It's a pose set up by
their benefactors: the good old KGB. The ones who
sprung 'em. Near as I've been able to find out, it
happened like this. . . ."

*More than a month earlier, February 14, Valentine's
Day.*

The elderly security guard at the gate didn't look

17

twice at the plumbing repair truck pulling into the drive of the Quentin County Home for the Mentally Disabled. The patients were always stuffing things into the toilets or breaking off pieces of pipe to use for clubs, and the repair truck was by now a common sight. So the guard pressed the button, let Death through in a white panel truck, and went back to reading *Game and Fishing* magazine.

He didn't notice that the truck stopped on the white-gravel drive only thirty yards inside the gate. He didn't see the man in the gray jumpsuit climb out the back and trudge back up to the gatehouse. He didn't notice anything unusual—till the man in the jumpsuit, one Uri Polonov, recently smuggled into the USA across the Canadian border, opened the door of the gatehouse, stepped inside, and closed it behind him. Then the guard looked up, smiling his puzzlement, and said, "Ain't got any pipes here to fix, son."

The smile melted when he saw the silenced Uzi in the "plumber's" hand. The machine pistol whispered about complacent old fools, and made its point with the steel-jacketed slugs that stitched red holes across the old man's chest.

The killer turned away. But before he went out the door, he hit the switch opening the gate. It might be necessary to leave the Quentin County Home quickly.

He returned to the truck. He didn't look back at the body of the old man on the floor.

The white panel truck drove down the long winding drive between the palm trees swaying faintly in the arid wind of the Mojave. The asylum was an oasis in the Southern California barrenness of Quentin County. Jerkily spuming sprinklers sissed jets of water over broad green lawns. A few of the more docile patients worked over tulip gardens bordering the white false-stucco administration building.

There were three men in the panel truck. Polonov in back, a Cuban named Julio Garcia in the passenger seat, and a man they called Martindale at the wheel. Martindale wasn't his real name—only certain high officials in the Politburo knew the name of this thoroughly Americanized KGB colonel. Americanized—but only in his speech, his mannerisms. Not in respect to his loyalties.

Martindale was the Soviet Union's number-one sabotage-and-subversion operative. His hair was comic-book-steely blue-black, his eyes china blue, his soft mouth always faintly smiling. His face had been refashioned in a Swiss hospital to a psychiatrist's specifications. It was designed to fit the "trustworthy-masculine-archetype" role. He had dimples and a magnetic smile. He could have been a model for *Gentlemen's Quarterly*— except now he wore a workman's jumpsuit embroidered with the name that was also freshly painted on the side of the panel truck: GANNON PLUMBING.

Garcia was a pudgy man with a hand-rolled cigarette in his liver-colored lips. He had a map of the asylum's grounds on his lap. "Hang a right here," he told Martindale. "Security ward is around back."

They swung around back, following a feeder road, and pulled up in the almost empty parking lot of the security ward, an L-shaped building with bars and heavy metal-mesh screens on its windows. The bars and mesh were painted a dull peach color, like the rest of the four-story building. The parking lot was in the crook of the L. A truck marked INSTITUTIONAL FOOD SUPPLY COMPANY was parked across the sidewalk from the glass doors.

Martindale pointed toward the doors. Garcia nodded.

A teenage boy, his long blond hair spilling over his plaid shirt, was coming through the sliding glass doors, his arms full of empty cardboard boxes. He whistled as he came.

Garcia got out the side door and walked to the outer wall of the building to one side of the glass doors, out of sight of the reception desk in the lobby. He stood in a bed of tulips, staring perplexedly at a dripping water faucet. In his right hand was a toolbox. He set the toolbox down between the tulips—careful not to crush them—and opened it. He took out a large monkey wrench. The delivery boy was just piling the cardboard boxes in the back of his truck. He slammed the door and walked toward the driver's-side door, glancing incuriously at the plumbing repair truck. Martindale had figured right: he was about to leave.

"Jesus Chris' ... son of a bitch!" Garcia swore loudly, bending over the faucet. He straightened and called out, "Hey, buddy!" over his shoulder at the delivery boy. "Can you give me a hand?"

"Sure!" the boy said cheerfully. He crossed the sidewalk. "You want me to hold the wrench or what?" He stepped into the tulip bed and bent over the faucet. "What's the—?" The rest was an inarticulate squawk as Garcia brained him with the wrench.

"Sorry, kid," Garcia mumbled around his cigarette as he dragged the body behind a clump of gardenias. "Got orders no one leaves while we're here. And you saw the truck." Garcia liked talking to the dead. He believed they listened, nodding understandingly in the next world.

Garcia returned to the truck. "Take the wheel," Martindale told him, climbing out. "Twenty minutes, then come check."

"Sure." Garcia had no trace of an accent. He'd been born and raised in New York City. He climbed into the truck, laying the toolbox on the engine cover beside him. Besides the monkey wrench, the toolbox contained a Uzi, a .45, ammunition, a smoke grenade, a packet of plastic explosives, and a detonator.

Martindale and Polonov carried toolboxes identical to Garcia's.

They carried them into the lobby.

A thick glass window with a speaking grid, like a cashier's window, was centered in the wall opposite the front entrance. To the right of the window was a locked metal door with a small wire-meshed glass in its upper half.

Martindale stepped to the speaker's grid in the admissions window. "Excuse me ... ?" he said, smiling.

Joan Ben Gurion looked up from her desk. Framed

in the admissions window was one of the most attractive male faces she'd ever seen. She tried to look impassive as she asked, "Yes?"

But that smile—it made her feel funny. In a nice way.

It got to be such a *drag* in Security—she was the only young woman there. The other nurses and attendants were at least fifty, and soured by years of dealing with hardcore inpatients.

And the men—the orderlies—*ugh*! They were either drunks, or drug addicts, or just plain stupid. The doctors? All married or too old.

She'd just been typing up some notes for Dr. Preston and making lots of mistakes because her mind was on something else. She was reliving—with herself as the principal actor—the first torrid love scene in *Flaming Hearts,* a historical romance by Patricia Soulbreath, which lay beside her desk in an imitation-leather book cover.

And the man in the window looked *so much* like Jesse in *Flaming Hearts* . . .

"We got a call about some plumbing problems here," the man said, his eyes twinkling at her.

Plumbing problems? He was a plumber? She was disappointed. She'd hoped he was an intern. A young, ambitious, unmarried intern. But then, plumbers did all right. . . .

She smiled coyly at him and said, "Oh, gee, I didn't hear about that, I'll have to check with the ward supervisor . . ." She reached for the phone.

But she stopped when he tapped on the window. She looked up. He was shaking his head.

"It wasn't the ward supervisor who called—it was State Health Department. It's a routine check, see. The state sent us . . ."

That was funny, she thought. First he'd said someone called about plumbing problems—then he changed the story.

Something in his eyes seemed to say: *It's you I'm here to see.*

Could it be that he'd seen her another time and had dropped in with this excuse to see her again? What else? Why should anyone in his right mind want to break *into* an asylum?

Trembling a little, brown-eyed, mousy Joan Ben Gurion stood up and went to press the button that unlocked the door from the lobby. As she pressed the button, the door gave out a buzzing sound. And as she heard the buzzing sound she thought: Oh, God, I hope I didn't make a mistake.

Because now she had another kind of funny feeling.

There were two plumbers, she saw now. And that wasn't usual.

They came through the door smiling. The dark one smiled like a movie star, and it was believable. But the other one, the one with the blond eyebrows—his smile was cut in ice.

Without thinking, she took a step back into her office cubby.

The pretty smile was carrying a toolbox. He stepped into the cubby with her, and there wasn't room for the other man.

"John Swenson," said the smiling plumber.

"Uh . . . how do you do."

"No, no—I'm looking for John Swenson. He's a patient here. Do you know where he is?"

"No." That was a lie. Swenson was notorious. Everyone knew about him. But now she was sure she'd made a mistake in letting these men in.

She was backed up against her desk; he was leaning over her so close she could smell his cologne.

He reached into his toolbox and came out with something squarish and heavy and black. It took her a second to realize it was a gun.

"Oh, no," she said.

"Yes," he said.

"Look, I can't let you see that guy—I mean, you're friends of his, right? So you want to let him out? I can't let you do that. He killed six people and he hasn't changed at all—"

"Are those the files for the patients in here?" He pointed to a filing cabinet jammed in the narrow space between the desk and the wall.

"Yes."

"Get Swenson's file. Hurry."

She went to the file, rummaged, and fingers fumbling, brought out a file folder. It was thick.

He took it, unbuttoned the top of his jumpsuit, and tucked it inside. He reached into the other side of the jumpsuit and from an interior pocket took a folded sheet of paper. He unfolded it and spread it out on her desk.

The paper said:

TO WHOM IT MAY CONCERN
John Swenson was framed to take the rap for killings performed by CIA flunkies! We, his brothers in the New Minds Liberation Army, are liberating him so he can carry on the work of the architects of World Revolution! Less than eight percent of the population controls ninety percent of the world's resources! The government has taken bread from the mouth of the poor! The NMLA is not afraid to kill for the sake of the class revolution!

And so forth.

She didn't read the rest because the terror took her then. The words blurred together into gray meaninglessness. It was the ski mask that did it. The man with the gun had put on a ski mask. That meant he expected some of the people here would see him and live. But she had seen him without the mask. Which meant . . .

"Take us to Swenson," said the ski mask. The yellow-browed man was taking a ski mask out of his pocket and putting it on, too.

"The floor orderly has the key, I don't—"

"Then take us to him."

"You're going to kill me," she said, feeling each word on her tongue as solid and thick as a lump of lead. It was an amazing thing to consider. " 'Cause I saw your face."

"Shut up and come on."

"I'll take you there and then you'll kill me!" Shriller. Her voice had a life of its own. She couldn't keep it inside her. *"You're going to kill me!"*

She was screaming it now, and it was just too loud.

"You're going to—"

"If you say so," Martindale muttered. The machine pistol hissed like a stammering python and the slugs picked her up and threw her over her desk; she fell sprawling, rattling a trashcan against the file cabinet; she shook a little, and lay still. Three of the bullets had passed through her, at that close range, and smashed into the paperback book beside the desk, tearing it apart. One of the pages fluttered through the air like an autumn leaf and came to rest on her shattered bosom. A finger of blood underlined the words: *"I'll love you forever, Jesse,"* she breathed. *"You can't stop me. I'll love you even if you kill me."*

Swenson knew with a psycho's certainty that the men with the ski masks and guns had come for him. Any other time he'd have been wrong, hallucinating through megalomaniacal paranoia. This time he was right.

He could see them through the small unbreakable glass window in the door of his room. He looked down the hallway, straining to see at the awkward angle, and made out the men with the ski masks through the glass that divided the ward dormitory from the third-floor admissions area. He saw something that at first seemed like a hallucination: a telephone floating through the air. A whole telephone. But then he realized that one of the men had torn it from the wall and thrown it through the air. It smashed against a wall. He saw the floor orderly, that ugly bastard March-willow, waving his arms, hysterical. The jerk had probably given the keys to his partner again, so he could open up the pantry—against the rules—to get the orderlies something to eat before dinner. So he didn't have the keys with him. So they'd have to . . .

They did! The glass exploded inward.

Oh, let it not be a dream, let it be true! Swenson thought.

And then his mind abruptly shifted directions, as happens with paranoids.

What if they had come to kill him? Maybe they'd been hired by the relatives of the pig people he'd carved up . . .

But then they were at his door, gesturing for him to get back behind the bed. They *were* here to help him!

He ran to the cot and tore the mattress off, pulled it over him, waited. Two minutes later the room shook with an explosion.

Bits of plaster pattered down from the ceiling, and then it was quiet. He climbed out from behind the mattress. A figure out of hell loomed up in the smoke, a hideous abstraction for a face. "Come on," said the stranger through the ski mask, "we're breaking you out of here."

Swenson cawed happily and walked out through the shattered door. He walked over the broken glass in the hallway, and saw Marchwillow lying in a pool of blood by the elevator. His stomach had been shot open. He was still alive, trying to stuff yards of entrails back into his blown gut.

Surging with an ecstatic sense of destiny, Swenson turned to the ski mask and demanded, "Let me use the gun on him!"

"Not yet," said the ski mask. "After your training. Your chance will come." Swenson's hellish savior turned to Marchwillow and casually shot him in the head.

Shivering with pleasure, Swenson allowed himself to be taken out the door.

Destiny, that's what it was, Swenson knew. It was his destiny to rule. To rearrange the world in his own image. To begin small—like Mao—and to get bigger and bigger, like Mao, like Stalin, like Hitler. But he wouldn't make the mistakes those others made. No, he'd be very very careful.

When he and his followers had killed the pig people for refusing to make the movie about his cause, he'd known that the police would get him for a while. But he knew also that his followers would liberate him. And his time imprisoned would be a legendary ordeal, a martyrdom that the poets would write about after he took over. After the big takeover. After he killed his enemies. After . . .

Esmeralda. He needed Esmeralda beside him. She helped him feel it.

"I got to have her," he told the man in the ski mask as they emerged from the building. He stopped him on the sidewalk to tell him.

"What? Stop babbling and get in the truck! Hurry!"

"Esmeralda! She's in Sunnybrook Sanatorium over in—"

"We know all about it. She is on the list. Another team is breaking her out. Now, get in the truck!"

Only after he was sitting in the back of the truck, trundling off through the parking lot, did it occur to Swenson to wonder: Who the hell *are* these guys?

Looking out his barred window, Herman "Santa Claus" Brewster saw the men with the guns and ski masks take Swenson into the truck. He saw the body lying in the bed of gardenias. Since he was actually Santa Claus, who believed in goodness, he tried to tell the orderly to call the police.

"Why should I call the cops?" the orderly asked, smiling.

Herman told him what he'd seen, and ended with, "It must have something to do with that explosion we heard!"

The orderly shook his head, laughing, and gave him some more Thorazine.

3

You Can't Beat the Country
for Peace, Quiet, and Murder

Sullivan and Knickian got out of the Checker cab and crossed the sidewalk to the doorway of Knickian's apartment building. The doorman saw Sullivan first, and backed away nervously. Then he saw Knickian and relaxed. He opened the door for them and they went in, took the elevator, and rode up to the fifth floor. All the time, Sullivan was silent, smoking. He hadn't said a thing during the cab ride from the bar. From time to time Knickian would look at him, start to speak, and then change his mind.

Sullivan would give his answer in his own good time.

Finally, in the hallway outside the door, Sullivan said, "I've got to know more."

"That's why we're here. You can see the files."

"No, I mean I've got to talk to someone in the family. Bremmer's family."

"His mother is your employer. An old lady—but feisty. She's putting up the money for your fee. You can talk to her."

"Okay. Tomorrow. Tonight I check the files out and

27

you give me your version of how you think the kidnapping . . . Wait a minute. Don't open the door."

Knickian took the key from the lock and stepped back, nodding. "You're right," he said softly. "I forgot about that. One of 'em got away."

He moved to one side of the door.

"Wait here," Sullivan said in a whisper. He went to the hallway window. There was a fire escape visible through the dusty glass. He unlocked the window, slid it upward, and stepped through onto the fire escape.

Ten minutes later, Knickian heard noises from within his apartment. He drew his gun and waited. The door opened from the inside.

Knickian flicked the safety off the .38 and cocked it. Sullivan stepped out of the apartment and grinned at him.

Knickian let out a long, relieved breath.

"It's clean," Sullivan said. "But we better not hang out here long. You can come over to my place."

"How'd you get in?"

"Down a pipe from the roof, jimmied the lock on your window. It wasn't much of a lock. Come on."

The two men went into the cluttered studio apartment. It smelled faintly rancid from moldering Kansas Fried Chicken lying half-eaten on paper plates. Knickian was a confirmed bachelor.

Knickian took a suitcase from the closet, opened it, and from a false bottom beneath an untidy heap of dirty laundry produced an envelope. He passed it to Sullivan. "This is everything I got on Swenson and his people and the NMLA. I'm not supposed to have taken the file out of the office, but if I hadn't, I figure it would've got shredded."

Sullivan was frowning. "Why, Knickian? Why would they use an uncontrollable nut like Swenson to set up their dummy 'revolutionary cell'?"

"I'm not sure. Except that crazies run a lot of terrorists groups—maybe they worked up a good technique for controlling them. And they make good fighters.

Suicidal. Also, there was some leftist controversy about Swenson's having been framed by the CIA—I figure they're exploiting that myth."

"Yeah. But there's got to be more."

Knickian was smiling, seeing the interest, the intense concentration on Sullivan's face as he thought it over.

Sullivan noticed Knickian's look and scowled. "Look, don't get yourself convinced I'm gonna take this job! I said we'd *talk*!"

But they both knew Sullivan was in. He smelled the blood of the enemy.

Knickian sat in a wicker chair on the terrace of Sullivan's Central Park West penthouse suite looking at the city lights. The dawn was coming up, translucent gray-blue, and the lights were losing their shine, beginning to pale into the general glow of morning. Knickian's .38 lay cold in his lap—just in case the KGB knew where Sullivan lived.

Sullivan, a cold cup of coffee at his elbow, sat at the dining-room table just inside the open French doors, reading through Knickian's files.

His eyes started to blur, and he forced them to focus as he read the transcripts of the statement by the housekeeper who'd survived the attack on the Bremmer country estate outside Arlington, Virginia.

Sullivan read:

". . . I knew they weren't delivering nothing. You don't get three deliverymen in one truck unless they're delivering, you know, a piano or something. So I tried to close the door on 'em and they kicked it in and pushed me back inside. Then I saw two women get out of the truck and run to cut the telephone wires. The men were foreign-looking, except for their leader, he was a real good-looking guy, and he even smiled at me. But there was nothing good in him, because of what happened after. He pushed me inside, and there was this other one, he was laughing part of the time, and I heard a woman—she was beautiful, like a Gypsy, with black hair down to her hips and big black eyes—she called him John. . . ."

Sullivan opened a folder beside the transcript and looked again at the glossy black-and-white prison photos. John Swenson, aka "The People's Messiah," age twenty-nine. Short brown hair, "wolfish" blue eyes, birthmark shaped roughly like a crucifix on underside of jaw right side of his face. Five feet, five inches. One hundred and forty-five pounds. Arrested at age seventeen for poisoning the neighbors' dogs; acquitted for lack of evidence. Arrested at eighteen for attempted rape; acquitted when the plaintiff left town, was unavailable for hearings. There were indications Swenson may have frightened her into going. Swenson went into the Navy at nineteen, dishonorably discharged a year later for his part in the beating of an Indonesian girl. Arrested on charges of dealing PCP, "angel dust," at age twenty. Escaped in transit. Reappeared under false name as leader of a Southern California political and semireligious cult two years later. After a local filmmaker refused to do a propaganda film on Swenson's movement, Swenson led an angel-dust-stoned raiding party that killed the filmmaker, his wife and child, and three business associates. It was a ritual killing, and the butchered victims were badly disfigured. There were indications the children had been tortured before . . .

Sullivan closed his eyes and shook his head. He felt the old anger coming. He forced himself to read the file on Swenson's lover, Esmeralda. Her picture was beside Swenson's—she stared with sultry defiance at the cop photographer. She was "beautiful, like a Gypsy, with black hair down to her hips and big black eyes." Her lips were a slash of bloodred and her nails long and red and sharp. She wore tight black dresses and saw herself as "Circe, and Hecate, the Witch Goddess." She killed her younger brother, setting him on fire, when he was eight and she was twelve. She went to a home for disturbed children for three years, was released as a result of good behavior at age fifteen, and almost immediately began hustling on Sunset Strip. She was arrested in connection with the murders of two out-of-town businessmen believed to have been her tricks, at age seventeen, but was released for lack of evidence. She was an inpatient at the Center for Drug Rehabilitation for heroin and cocaine abuse at nineteen. Three arrests for shoplifting, two for prostitution, one for possession of a controlled substance. She became high priestess of the People's Messiah cult in 1980 and allegedly was involved in a drug-dealing conspiracy with Swenson and Jeffrey "Bloodsucker" Gordon. Esmeralda Wheland, Swenson, Gordon, and a Spaniard known only as Ortega—another cultist about whom little is known—were helped to escape from their respective incarcerations in February of ...

"What a bunch of winners," Sullivan muttered. He returned to the housekeeper's statement: "The kids were in the game room playing video games, and Mr. Bremmer, he was in his den working, Mrs. Bremmer was getting ready for her tennis lesson and their daughter, Miss June, was packing for vacation. There were two kids—Benny Bremmer, he was eleven, and Angela, Mr. Bremmer's niece, she was thirteen. God, she was a lovely child. And I tried to run past these guys at the door, to get the police, and that's when I saw the guns. I don't know why I didn't notice 'em before—maybe because that good-looking one, his face just caught your interest. His smile. And when I tried to run past them, they shot at me. I guess one of the bullets hit me in the head, but not directly, and it only *looked* like I was hurt bad. So when I fell down, I wasn't dead—I was just sort of stunned. But they thought I was dead. Then Mr. Bremmer, Mrs. Bremmer, and Miss June come running out together—I was seeing this from down on the floor, like I was seeing something in a dream—and Mrs. Bremmer screamed and tried to run ... so that girl shot her." The transcript noted that here the housekeeper broke down and wept. She recovered and went on: "So then this guy with the pretty smile stopped smiling, started yelling at the Gypsy girl, saying she'd killed a valuable hostage. And something about obeying orders. And then the Gypsy girl went downstairs with that Spanish guy and I heard the kids screaming."

Sullivan sat back in his chair and shook his head. Knickian came in and looked at him questioningly.

"I'm in," Sullivan said, making it official.

4

The Old Lady and
the Hired Killer

Grandmother Bremmer's suite on Sutton Place was furnished with French antiques. There were a great many things of lace and delicate glass figurines, and the rococo chairs looked as if they would not hold a big man's weight. Sullivan felt a little uncomfortable there and more than a little out of place. Knickian, unshaved, in a rumpled suit, sat in a love seat across a crystal-topped coffee table from Sullivan; he looked equally out of place. Sullivan resisted the impulse to light a cigarette. There were no ashtrays.

To take his mind off cigarettes Sullivan said, "the Knickian, the guy you got the information about the break-in at the asylum from—how'd he find out so much about how it happened?"

"He was in Swenson's cult. He was one of the guys Polonov and Martindale broke out. That's how he learned their names. He was ready to give a deposition to the DIA when he killed himself—or rather, when somebody made it look like he killed himself. And only myself and a few people in the DIA, including the mole, knew where he was."

"Who's the mole?"

33

"Calls himself McCarter. I think he was taken to
the USSR for undercover training in 1961. But I can't
prove it—and the CIA won't listen to me. McCarter's
got me blacklisted as a nut—"

"Mr. Sullivan?" said the maid, a Hispanic girl with
a slight accent.

She came briskly into the room as she spoke.

"Yeah," Sullivan said.

"Mrs. Bremmer will see you now."

"Right. Come on, Knickian."

"Uh . . . I'll wait here, Jack."

Sullivan shot him a bitter look and went nervously
into the hall and out to the terrace to meet the woman
who was to pay his fee: the eighty-two-year-old phil-
anthropic liberal socialite. Not typical of Sullivan's
usual clientele.

But then, since he'd gone out of ordinary military-
mercenary work, he had no "usual clientele." Anyone
who had a just reason to want vengeance was his
client. And evil can reach into any life, can hurt
anyone at all. But Sullivan had noted that it seemed
to prefer hurting the defenseless, the innocent, the
decent.

The old woman who met him on the terrace was
dignified and poised—but she'd clearly been hurt by
something. Deeply hurt. Her eyes showed a stoic
battle against emotional pain.

It was late afternoon. A ragged troop of clouds rode
lazily in the gray-blue sky. Terraced buildings stood
like art-deco ziggurats on every side; bone-white sky-
scrapers rose in the distance. The city hummed from
the streets below. The air was fresh, the terrace damp
from rain an hour ago.

Celia Bremmer's tea table, however, was perfectly
dry, and laid out with cakes and teas, British-style.
The old woman sat ramrod straight on the other side
of an ornate silver service. She wore a black dress suit
and a black scarf. Her face was narrow, pale, and
drawn, but there were traces of the beauty she'd known
as a young woman. Sullivan was a little bit in awe of

her. He eased his weight-lifter's bulk cautiously onto the fragile-seeming chair by the glass tabletop when she said, "Please sit, Mr. Sullivan."

The chair squeaked ominously, but held him.

"Tea, Mr. Sullivan?"

"Uh ..." He hated tea. But ... "Yes, ma'am."

"You're a very polite young man. Would you prefer a shot of whiskey?"

"Yes, ma'am, to be honest."

"I'm having a little in my tea ... I just happen to have some in this flask. Here you are."

After they'd each sipped their drinks, she set her teacup down decisively and passed him an envelope. He opened it and read a message typed in capital letters:

BREMMER IS PART OF THE MILITARY-INDUSTRIAL COMPLEX THAT CONTROLS AMERICA AND IS SPREADING ITS IMPERIAL-ISTIC TENTACLES AROUND THE WORLD. BREMMER AND PEO-PLE LIKE HIM WILL BE MADE TO PAY. IF YOU WANT TO SEE HIM AND HIS DAUGHTER ALIVE AGAIN, GET FIVE MILLION DOL-LARS IN UNMARKED BILLS TOGETHER. PLACE AN AD IN THE PERSONALS SECTION OF THE SUNDAY NEW YORK TIMES SAY-ING "WE ACCEPT, FRIENDS OF B" AND YOU WILL BE CON-TACTED AGAIN ABOUT EXCHANGE OF MONEY FOR YOUR FAMILY. DO NOT SHOW THIS TO THE POLICE, AND DO PRE-CISELY AS YOU ARE TOLD, OR YOUR FAMILY WILL DIE. THIS MONEY WILL BE USED TO SUBSIDIZE THE REVOLUTION!

"Revolution!" Sullivan snorted, shaking his head. " 'The people' are the last thing they care about."

"I'm sure you're right, Mr. Sullivan. I also do not believe that these madmen will return my son and granddaughter alive. But I am trying to obtain the money from Bremmer Inc. I'm on the board, the company will pay, I think. In the meantime, before Sunday—if you care to accept the job—perhaps you can locate them."

"I have to ask you: *precisely* what do you want me to do?"

She sighed. "Is it necessary to spell it out?"

"Yes, ma'am."

"I want you to find these people and kill them. I do not trust the police to find them or to keep them if they do find them. I want to see to it that justice is done. I trust that you will do it very carefully—in the hopes you can get my son and granddaughter out alive, of course. But I think that is . . ." She shook her head. "Those people were Death," she finished huskily. "I spent the second part of my lifetime trying to help people like that—providing free psychiatric help for the mentally disturbed. And now . . ." She took another sip of her whiskey-laced tea, and the cup shook slightly in her hand. "I can offer you one hundred and fifty thousand dollars, Mr. Sullivan. I can get you half of it up front."

"Thanks. That'll help when it comes to buying—"

"I don't want to know, Mr. Sullivan. Ah . . . have you any idea where to begin looking?"

"An hour ago Knickian got a call from a friend of his at the state police, a guy named Fallen, offered to help us out unofficially. Fallen says a truck fitting the description given to us by your son's housekeeper was found abandoned in the countryside up near Rye. I think they may be up there. And there are other leads. If we can interrogate a KGB agent—"

"I don't want to know about that either, Mr. Sullivan." She rose, and when he'd carefully risen too, shook his hand. "I'll see the money gets to you through Mr. Knickian. He was—is, I hope—a friend of my son's. He's been a good friend. So, then, you officially take the job?"

"I . . ." He cleared his throat. "I'm honored to do it, ma'am."

She smiled, and amazed him by saying, "It's nice to meet a man with balls." And then, leaning on her cane, she tottered off to take a nap.

Milner felt strange holding the gun. It was a submachine gun. It felt all wrong in his hands.

He was used to guns, all right. He'd been an infantryman in Nam, and earned a Bronze Star—before the capture. Before the torture and the New Perspective. Before they showed him that Communism was the Way. But somehow he associated this gun with the time before that turning, when he'd been a sergeant in the U.S. Army. And it felt all wrong.

He started, hearing the crunch of bootsteps behind him, and spun, raising the SMG.

But it was only Polonov, looking faintly disgusted. "Do not play games with this weapon," he said, pushing the gun barrel aside.

"Sorry—guess I'm nervous out here. I'm still thinking about the damn truck. If someone finds it and—"

"No one saw us come and go in it. No one but those who are tied up here and those who are dead."

"We can't be sure of that. I think we ought to hire a boat, go up the coast—"

"Martindale will decide."

Milner snorted and shook his head. He turned away and looked again at the woods outside the decrepit farmhouse they'd chosen as their lying-low place. It was a misty dusk, wreaths of fog oozing slowly through the birch and elm trees, drops plip-plipping from branches into the mulch and newly sprouting ferns.

"I believe you are one of those who are not sure Martindale is making the correct decisions," Polonov said in his perfect but labored English.

"I just don't understand why we had to use those *nuts*. They got completely out of control. There was no reason to kill those kids. That asshole Swenson doesn't care about the revolution—he's just glory-hounding."

Polonov surprised Milner by saying, "I think maybe I agree with you. But Martindale thinks they will be great fighters. He believes they are also more expendable than a conventional cadre. And he thinks there is propaganda value in this Swenson—there are people in your American counterculture who regard him as a martyr. But Martindale has, I think, other plans for them."

"He's crazy himself to think he can control them."

Polonov shrugged. "Despite what your American President may think, we do not have direct control over the activities of the genuine American leftist guerrillas—not in North America. So we had to create our own. Ordinary mercenaries would not do what Martindale needed done. Bremmer had to be silenced."

"How will they launder the ransom money for revolutionary use?"

Polonov smiled. "Martindale has his connections. He does not share them with me."

Milner frowned. "Then how will we know the money will be used for the revolution? That's a lot of money."

Ignoring Milner's question, Polonov said, "Yes. A lot of money." He lit a Marlboro. "American cigarettes are overrated," he muttered. He hooked a thumb at the house. "Go on, I'm relieving you."

"Relieving" was the right word; relief was what Milner felt as he left the forbidding woods and trudged across the wet knee-high grass to the house. It was a two-story house, stained by the weather to an almost uniform dingy brown. The front part extended out in a single story and a sagging porch roof; the back rose to a high A-frame. The windows were boarded over. Light starred through chinks in the upper-floor windows. Martindale had rented the place for a month, pretending to be a bird-watcher camping out in a sleeping bag there. He'd made the rounds of the neighbors alone, armed only with binoculars and bird-spotting guide, just to let them know he'd be there. He didn't want anyone reporting suspicious strangers to the local sheriff. And no one had been surprised: there was a large bird sanctuary nearby, and bird-watchers came from all over the country to view the herons in the marshes beside the ocean. The bird-watchers were a familiar sight, and a source of local amusement. The nearest town, with about a thousand inhabitants, was Lightning Corners, about a quarter-mile from Singer Beach and Bird Sanctuary.

The front door of the house was boarded over. His legs cold from the wet soaking through his fatigues, Milner followed a faint path around the side of the house to the back. The back porch was missing; you could see the lighter places on the wood of the backwall where it had been. A few crooked nails still stuck out there. Evidently someone had torn it off, cannibalized it for firewood. Or maybe to build a chicken coop. Things happened, from time to time, in Lightning Corners: chicken coops were built.

But gangs of international spies and escaped lunatics holding millionaire industrialists for ransom? Look elsewhere for that, stranger. All we've got here are bird-watchers.

Letting these ironies play through his mind, Milner jumped up to the back door frame—there were no steps—and tapped three times short, two long, before entering.

Despite the signal, Garcia had his SMG leveled at Milner till he could see him clearly. Milner stepped into the greater light of the kerosene lamp on the splintery table beside the stove, and Garcia nodded, lowered the gun. The hand-rolled cigarette in the Cuban's liverish lips tilted down too, as if it had been prepared to fire had Milner been a hostile.

Garcia leaned back in the squeaking chair, swore as it jiggled, nearly collapsing under him. He steadied its wobbly legs with one hand, the other cradling the SMG against his plump middle.

"Where's Martindale?" Milner asked.

"Upstairs keeping an eye on the future Castro and his little Guevaras," Garcia said in a confidential tone. "Hey, chee, man, it's cold in here, uh? You think we should build a fire?"

"I'll ask Martindale."

He was grateful for an excuse to talk to Martindale. He felt an unease he couldn't quite focus in on. Martindale knew how to reassure him. He was a lot like Xai Chih. Chih had been his guide to the New Perspective after he'd been captured. All soft paternal smiles and patience, and with a parable from the writings of Ho Chi Minh for every doubting question.

Milner took a pocket flashlight from his jacket, and in its watery light climbed the narrow, musty stairway to the second floor. He stepped carefully over the missing fourth and seventh steps.

At the top of the steps he heard a girl scream.

He stopped, shivering, and it wasn't just the damp this time. Chih seemed a long way away.

He forced himself to go on.

There were three rooms on the top floor. On the right, through the open door, Milner could see Martindale bent over a pad and codebook, earphones on his head, jotting a message from the shortwave. This was no time to disturb him. Milner went a few steps farther and looked in the dimly lit room to the left.

The nineteen-year-old girl, June Bremmer, lay tied to the ancient box-spring mattress on the in-leaning four-poster that was the square room's only furnishing. Bremmer himself was sitting on the floor of the foot of the bed, tied to its frame. He was gagged, and even in the thin light from the flickering Coleman lantern Milner could see he was pallid from fear and horror.

Swenson leaned nonchalantly against the wall, smoking, and watching the bed with slitted eyes, smiling distantly. He looked up as Milner appeared in the door, and the smile was gone like a frightened housefly.

Bloodsucker Gordon knelt beside the bed, holding the lantern high over the frightened girl's face, grinning like a panting dog. He was the most obviously demented of the group; he even drooled from a corner of his lipless mouth from time to time. He was a matted-haired hippie with a nose that was noticeably crooked from having been broken; he was missing three teeth in front. Esmeralda was on the far side of the bed, leaning over the girl, whispering to her, whispering the things that made June Bremmer whimper and scream. "After we do that thing with the rat to your insides, we might let you watch when we take your dad to the . . ." She broke off at a grunt of warning from Swenson and looked up, her large liquid brown-black eyes catching the light like obsidian, glinting cold as black crystal. She was pale and raven-haired, her nose slightly hooked, her lips full and red. Her expression was sweet, like a mother affectionately telling her child a bedtime story.

Swenson had a .45 in his hand. He raised it, but didn't point it at Milner. Raising it was enough.

"What do you want, Mr. Milner, sir?" he asked with mock respectfulness. Gordon giggled idiotically.

"I think . . ." Milner broke off, a little shaken by the sight of three lunatics gazing at him with outright hostility. Where was the fourth—Ortega? It made him nervous not knowing. Ortega was always quiet. And that quiet was scarier than Gordon's overt dementia.

Milner forced himself to speak. "I think you should leave them alone. They're useful, but if you make her . . ." He couldn't bring himself to say "crazy" in the present company. "If you get her hysterical she won't be any good when it comes time for her to give a phone message. The old lady won't deal if the girl's not able to talk. They've got to know she and her father are alive."

"We didn't do nothing to her," Gordon said, making a slobbery-sucking sound after speaking, as he always did.

"It's possible to frighten people to death," Milner said.

"I know the moment of their deaths," Esmeralda said with her usual pseudo-cosmic melodrama. "They won't die that way. I've seen how they'll die."

"If we can convert Bremmer, we won't have to kill him," Milner said. But it rang false, even in his own ears.

He glanced at the Bremmer girl. Blond, tanned, athletic, very much a debutante—or had been. Now she was bruised, and sobbing, her bathrobe torn and blood-spotted. Her father was a white-haired stocky man with a face marked by years of authority. But all the toughness had drained away; he was a frightened old man now.

Milner looked away from them. He must not get personally involved. He had to see them as symbols—the millionaire exploitationist capitalist, the union-buster, the decadent daughter—not as people.

And was he to see these psycho killers still in their institutional blues as ... Freedom fighters? Guerrillas struggling for the cause?

Gordon had a screwdriver in his hand; he'd found it in a corner of the kitchen. It was sharp and rusty. He ran it along the girl's rib cage, scraping, not quite hard enough to gouge—yet. Gordon made a high sound like *pee-huh pee-huh pee-huh* in his throat that was his version of laughter.

Milner found himself acting against his own common sense. He raised his submachine gun. "Get away from her," he said. He tilted the gun toward Swenson. "Tell them. And drop the guns."

Muscles jumped in Swenson's jaws, and he tensed. But he dropped the gun.

He was a small man, with a punky thatch of brown hair and strangely delicate features. He smiled, as if unconcerned. "Back off, my children," he said.

"I've seen your end too, Milner," said Esmeralda, backing away from the bed. "I've seen Mr. Milner dying slowly ..."

"Shut up," Milner hissed. He'd heard someone walking down the hall.

He stepped farther into the room and moved to one side of the door, flattening there, making a warning gesture to the others: *silence.*

Ortega stepped through the door, SMG dangling at the end of his right arm. Milner pressed the muzzle of his own machine pistol to the back of Ortega's head and snarled, "Drop that weapon." The Uzi clattered to the floor.

Ortega was tall and stooped, his shoulder blades almost like wings protruding from his back. He was shaved bald, had even shaved off his eyebrows; his hawk nose was missing one nostril, torn raggedly away in some fight. He darted his dark eyes at Milner and grinned.

"Okay," Milner said, "now go on out into the hall—all of you."

The four NMLA members trooped into the hall. Gordon giggled as he went, pretending to march.

"Please," said the girl on the bed, "you're going to let us go now, aren't you? You're going to help us, right? You're not like—"

"Shut up!" Milner barked at her. "You're prisoners of the New Mind Liberation Army! You're . . . you're political prisoners. You've been living on the backs of the workers for years, and you're going to pay for it now! All I'm doing is seeing that valuable hostages are—"

"*Is* that all you're doing, my friend?" Martindale's voice.

Milner turned convulsively. "Uh . . ." Martindale was standing in the doorway, the four loonies behind him, all four of them grinning.

Milner swallowed. "Yeah, I'm just . . . They were torturing her. She's got to sound like she's sane and safe when she gives the phone message. You yourself warned them once to leave her alone."

He didn't like the way Martindale was smiling at him. The man hadn't even bothered to bring along a weapon.

But now Martindale nodded. "I see." He turned to Swenson. "Don't go near the prisoners again, unless I tell you to. Stand a guard outside the door."

Swenson frowned. "Now, look, we're not your trained animals, man. We . . ." He let the protest trail off, seeing something on Martindale's face. Something that must have reassured him, judging by his grin. "Okay," he said.

Martindale said, "Milner, come along with me, please."

Milner followed the Russian agent to the room containing the radio. Martindale sat in the chair and laid a hand on the message he'd decoded on the sheet. "There's a man who's interfering with our attempts to get rid of this Knickian. We have reason to believe he may be looking for us. I have a suspicion who he might be, judging from the description. When you were in Vietnam—when you were still fighting for the South—did you hear anything about a man called the Specialist?"

Milner shrugged. "Sure. He was supposed to be some gung-ho working out of a Special Forces advance-recon team. I heard a story about how he got his nickname."

"What story was that?"

"Well . . . they say he was always volunteering for special missions no matter what they were. They'd ask for a specialist in HALO drops, and he'd step forward. They'd ask for a specialist in sniping, and out he'd jump. So one day his C.O. said something like, 'How can you be a specialist in anything when you do it *all*?' And the guy said, 'Sir, there's only one thing I specialize in—killing the enemy.' Or words to that effect."

Martindale sighed. He looked tired. "I think it may be the same man. Do you remember his name?"

"Something Irish."

"Sullivan?"

"Yeah, that was it."

Martindale shook his head. "I was afraid of that." He looked up at something over Milner's shoulder. "Well, if that's who it is, we may need all the help we can get. Unfortunately, though, we'll have to do without *you*."

Martindale nodded to someone Milner couldn't see. Milner turned—and a gun barrel sliced down on his forehead. The room exploded with sparks, and he was falling.

He came to himself a few moments later, lying in a sodden heap on the floor, stunned, temporarily unable to make his muscles respond to his mental commands. *Run*! he told them. *Get up and run*!

Martindale's voice came from across interstellar space: "I'm afraid our Milner is no longer trustworthy. I've been running men for a long time, and I know when one turns. You can see it in his eyes. Another day and he would have slipped off and turned us in."

Milner realized then that Martindale was right. He had already decided, inside somewhere, that this operation was a farce. That it was a betrayal of his cause. That it would have to be stopped.

"What we do with him?" Ortega's voice, something Milner had heard only once before.

"Take him out into the woods, shoot him—one shot, for minimal noise—and bury him. Now."

5

Two Hunts Become One

The fat man shifting nervously in the chair—a wicker chair just a little too small for him—flicked his eyes at Sullivan and then forced them away. He seemed to be both frightened and fascinated by Sullivan.

Sullivan smiled, trying to reassure him. "Take it easy, Mr. Binder. We're all on the same side here. How about telling me the part where you became suspicious of Milner. I read Knickian's report, but it's a little foggy in places."

Knickian was perched on a stool by the breakfast bar in Sullivan's Manhattan penthouse. It was seven P.M.; the city lights were coming alive outside.

Binder was a round man in absurdly oversized aviator glasses and a yellow leisure suit. Sweat beaded on his red cheeks. His piggish blue eyes blinked. "I worked as an assistant to both Milner and Bremmer," he said. He shifted again in the chair, and it creakcd piteously. "Mr. Bremmer was worried about the new government contract we had—we were doing the electronics guidance system for a new kind of missile. But it just wasn't testing out. The Army Chief of Staff, you know, said—oh, back a year or so—that, uh, it was shoddy

46

workmanship, all the problems with the MX and the cruise missiles and our new one. But Bremmer began to think it might be some kind of subtle sabotage. Russian agents on the assembly line fixing parts so they'd come loose under stress. So he asked Milner, his assistant, to commission a study on possible sabotage. I never trusted Milner, because he got his job through string-pulling. A guy in the Defense Intelligence Agency name of McCarter arranged the job."

Sullivan and Knickian looked at each other. McCarter was the man Knickian believed to be a Soviet mole in the agency.

"When they get their jobs through string-pulling instead of through merit, well, you just can't trust them to be competent," Binder was saying pettishly.

Sullivan suspected that Binder's dislike of Milner was both personal and professional. Milner had gotten the job Binder should have had, through "string-pulling" instead of coming up through the ranks by gradual promotion, and Binder resented it. That made Binder's testimony suspect. But then, as Binder went on, the parts fell into place, and Sullivan believed that despite the man's prejudice, he was probably right about Milner.

"So anyway," Binder went on, wheezing between sentences, "Bremmer commissioned a study through Bremmer Electronics Security Department, to look for evidence of subtle sabotage. The study found that there was plenty of opportunity, and though there was no concrete proof, it suggested that sabotage was a strong possibility. Well, I found out that Milner intercepted this report before it got to Bremmer's office and edited it, made it sound as if there was no sabotage indicated at all." His voice became self-righteous, his face redder. "Well, I went straight to Mr. Bremmer and laid it out for him. He called Milner out on the rug, and Milner claimed it all was a misunderstanding, he'd only eliminated certain 'hysterical excesses.' Bremmer fired Milner—which I thought was a mistake. He should have put a watch on him and caught him at something. And then Bremmer decided he would go before the Senate Subcommitte on Espionage and tell them he thought the damage to our guidance systems was subtle sabotage. And three weeks later, when he was getting ready for it, he was kidnapped. The day before he was scheduled to testify. And the material he was going to use in testimony disappeared. And then I was fired—and I thought Milner and McCarter were behind my getting fired. So I hired some private investigators to look into Milner's background. There was a lot that was covered up, but his ex-wife told us the truth. We found the records. He was a deserter in Nam. Well, actually he was captured, and then went through some kind of brainwashing. Anyway, he came out of it a Communist. And then he was secretly returned to the United States, and ended up working for Bremmer. I assume he was still a Communist, and overseeing all this sabotage."

Knickian took a glossy black-and-white photo from an envelope and laid it on the coffee table before Binder. "Do you know this man?"

"That's Milner—but younger," Binder said.

"And this is him now?" Knickian asked, putting another photo down. It was a picture of a man with a squarish face, secretive eyes, black hair balding, a stub of a nose.

'That's right."

"Have your private investigators found out where he is now?" Sullivan asked.

"No. I've given Mr. Knickian everything I have on him."

"Okay. Are you willing to testify," Knickian asked, looking Binder in the eye, "in court?"

Binder nodded eagerly.

Sullivan stood. "Okay. We'd better get him to some friends of mine in the FBI. They'll hide him till we can arrange testimony. The protection will have to be unofficial—they don't like conflicting with McCarter. Let's go."

Five minutes later they were ushering Binder

through the lobby of the apartment building, Knickian reassuring him. "You'll be perfectly comfortable, you'll be well-guarded, you'll be well-fed—don't worry. We can get your wife and bring her there—"

Binder stood stock-still. "What! Then I refuse!"

"Okay, okay, we won't tell your wife where you are."

"Thank God. She's been trying to make me diet." Binder shuddered. "What sort of cook do they—?" He broke off, staring. "Who are these people?"

He was referring to the four men converging on them as they stepped onto the sidewalk beneath the building's front-entrance awning.

Sullivan drew his gun—he was carrying a .357 Colt now, having decided the job needed "heavy artillery"— and stepped in front of Binder. But the four men had the drop on them. They had their pistols aimed at Sullivan's brisket and Knickian's chest. One of them flashed a badge. "DIA," he said. "This guy"—he nodded toward the quaking fat man—"goes with us."

"Bullshit," said Sullivan.

He cocked his gun.

The man with the badge looked at Sullivan. Sullivan stared back. He was a tall, gray-faced man with a squint. He licked his lips. "I said we're from—"

"That's bullshit too," said Knickian. "I'm from the DIA. I don't know you guys. Tell you what. Let's call the DIA office and ask them to send someone to sort it out."

The man licked his lips twice more, then glanced uncertainly at his companions. He had Sullivan out-gunned—but he was reluctant to begin blasting away on Central Park West.

Sullivan, for his part, was trying to make up his mind about the authenticity of these characters. Maybe they *were* from the Defense Department's intelligence service. If they were, and if he had to shoot his way through them, it would run counter to everything he believed in. But if they were on the level, if the badge wasn't a fake, chances were they'd been sent by

McCarter. Unknowingly they were therefore on a mission for the KGB.

"Okay," said the gray-faced guy with the badge, "we'll go into the lobby there and call in." He looked at Knickian. "We work mostly out of Washington—that's why you don't know us. But I know who *you* are, Knickian."

Knickian began to back through the electric-eye doors. The doors shooshed apart. Sullivan backed too, Binder stumbling with him. The four agents made as if to come in after them—but Sullivan stepped to one side, aimed at the housing containing the door's electric eye, and squeezed the trigger. The big gun roared and the housing shattered. The doors slammed shut and stayed shut. The agents banged on the glass as Sullivan and Knickian prodded the puffing Binder to the elevators. There was no back way out—they'd have to go up to the roof and over to another building.

If they turned their only witness over to McCarter, Binder would probably "disappear." They had to get him clear.

They heard gunshots and glass shattering behind them as the elevator doors closed. Two minutes later they stepped out of the elevator, and Sullivan unlocked the entrance to the penthouse. He urged Binder through—it was like riding herd on some overfed barnyard animal—and ran ahead of him to the terrace.

He opened the glass doors and went to the ladder leading to the adjacent roof to reconnoiter.

Knickian was close behind him. Binder was . . .

Where was Binder?

Halfway up the ladder, Sullivan looked over his shoulder, shouting at Knickian, "Keep your eye on him!"

That's when he saw the three men coming off the fire escape. They were running toward Binder. Sullivan turned and leapt from the ladder, fell four feet to the terrace, and bouncing on the balls of his feet, came up firing the .357. This time he had no hesitation in firing—the three men here weren't the DIA.

They were some KGB backup crew sent by McCarter; Sullivan recognized one of them.

That was the first one he shot, smashing a heavy-gauge tumbler through the Soviet's chest, making a blood-spuming hole big as a baseball as the man flopped over backward, gun discharging into the air. The other two had closed in on Binder, who was stumbling back, arms windmilling, toward the edge of the roof.

Sullivan couldn't hit them without hitting Binder too. They were on the other side of the terrace from him, thirty feet off. Knickian was struggling with a fourth man who'd come from within the apartment.

Sullivan ran toward the two dark-suited men wrestling Binder toward the abyss.

And then Binder shrieked; his shiny shoes flashed in the air, and he was gone, tumbling thirty stories down to make an ugly splash on the hood of a Cadillac. Destroying the car and himself.

Sullivan, enraged, snapped off four shots. The big gun roared in his hand, bucking with its eagerness, spitting flame. The two killers went spinning in opposite directions, arms flapping like shirt sleeves on a wind-blown drying line, huge red chunks torn out of them, two apiece, in the head and chest.

Sullivan skidded to a halt, stood over the bodies, breathing hard, shaking with anger.

He turned to Knickian and saw him standing over his assailant, gasping. There was a spreading stain of red at Knickian's right shoulder.

"You hurt bad?" Sullivan asked dully.

Knickian shook his head. "Grazed. We lost him?"

Sullivan nodded. "And we're gonna have a wonderful time explaining to the cops."

"Maybe I can help you explain some of it," said a voice from behind. Sullivan turned, gun at ready. It was the DIA agent and his three cronies. He ignored Sullivan's Colt and came over to look at the bodies. He shook his head. "What a mess."

"Your goddamn fault," Knickian growled, sinking into a deck chair.

"That right?" the agent asked sarcastically.

"You see what happened?" Sullivan asked.

The agent nodded. "I saw 'em push the fat guy over. I got here just in time for that. I know this one here." He prodded a white-faced corpse with his toe. "This is Orlov. Soviet agent. Guess they wanted that fat boy too."

"They and your boss McCarter are one and the same, goddammit!" Knickian snapped.

The agent grinned. "I've heard about your crackpot theories, Knickian." He shrugged. "Well, you guys ain't to blame for this mess anyway—these guys were clearly intruders. I'll testify to that much."

"Oh, thanks," said Knickian with heavy irony. "Yeah, thanks a lot."

But Sullivan was already thinking about the next move, now that the Binder ploy was blown. He had to find Milner. He had to hunt him down.

Milner was playing possum.

He'd lain limply in the room in which they'd struck him down, letting them think he was out cold.

Now Ortega and Gordon carried him through the woods, slung between them like two men with a rolled-up rug. They were looking for a secluded-enough spot. Ferns and moss and dewy spiderwebs streaked Milner's cheeks and neck as the two psycho killers carried him through the underbrush. Ortega had him by the ankles, Gordon under the arms. His head lolled. He felt the sharp-edged leaf of a wild holly bush draw a cold line across one side of his throat as he was dragged past it, as if it were tracing the place where a knife could slash his life away.

No: a bullet. Martindale wanted to be sure he didn't accidentally survive. A bullet in the head. No mistakes. They'd shoot him between the eyes, point-blank, scrape out a shallow grave with knives, and cover him over.

Milner wished he weren't an atheist. You can't pray to Marx or Mao.

"This is good enough," Gordon said. "I'm tired."

Ortega grunted assent and they let go of Milner.

Milner had only a fraction of a second to react. His head banged with pain and he felt nauseated and weak. But he had to do it now, in that split second before he hit the ground.

He twisted, fell on his side, rolled, got his feet under him. He heard the sound of a gun cocking, Gordon swearing; he glimpsed Ortega looming up in front of him.

Rushing on adrenaline, Milner sprang at Ortega, hitting him in a football block, knocking him down before the surprised killer got his SMG unslung.

"Git outta the way dammit, Ortega!" Gordon yelled, trying to get a clear shot at Milner. But it was dark in the woods, and Ortega had been carrying the lantern. Milner was on his feet again, leaping over Ortega. The Hispanic made a grab at his ankles and caught only the hem of his fatigues. Milner jerked loose and kept going, pounding across the wet mulch, zigzagging, a cold sensation in the midst of his back where he expected any second to feel the slugs rip into him. The gun barked behind him, and his heart leapt. A tree beside him spat bits of its bark at his cheek, and then he was behind it, still running, putting more trees between him and the two men coming after him. Another spray of bullets went slicing through the air and he felt a tugging and an icy sensation in his right thigh, just under the buttock. He'd been hit. He ignored it, and prayed—forgetting his atheism—that the leg wouldn't give out under him. It kept pumping away, though a bit wobbly now.

The tree trunks were streaks of gray-black against the blue-green dimness; here and there the tops of bushes and tree-limbs were picked out by the failing light, pink and gold. Night-flying insects danced at his face and away. The air seemed sticky and thick as he went on, like he was plowing through syrup, and

he realized he was growing weak from loss of blood.
He could hear the psycho killers behind him, crashing
through brush, Gordon swearing at him; when he
risked a glance over his shoulder, he saw the lantern
swinging like a drunk comet between the trees, maybe
forty feet back. He had a pretty good lead on them—
must have lost them for a while. They'd stopped firing.
Someone might hear it and call the sheriff.

Suddenly he broke from a screen of shrubbery into
an open meadow. On the far side of the meadow was a
barbed-wire fence, a silhouette like bars of dirge music,
and beyond that the dead yellow stubble of last year's
cornfield. He staggered toward the fence, reached it
gasping, leaned for ten precious seconds against a
weather-ragged wooden post, his heart banging through
his chest, breath like knives in his lungs. He forced
himself to climb over the fence, thinking: *Careful. Not
too hasty. This is critical. Get tangled in this wire and
they've got you.* He felt barbs tear cloth and rake skin,
and then he was over and jogging unevenly at right
angles to his previous course, following the fence down-
hill through the thickening darkness toward the black
lump on the flatland at the bottom of the slope. He
took the black lump to be a barn. His wounded leg had
gotten over its shock, was beginning to send searing
waves of pain up into him, threatening to paralyze him.
He forced himself on, each jog becoming a single-
minded effort. The barn seemed to get no nearer.

The darkness and the slope worked in his favor; at
first the ones hunting him didn't see him when they
came to the fence.

He was halfway to the barn before they spotted him
and came after.

He ground his teeth against the pain and forced
himself to slog on through the soft dirt. It was too
soft, and on the verge of being mud. It sucked at his
ankles as if trying to hold him back.

Then the barn loomed over him.

He hobbled around its corner, went in through a
side door. Manure scents. Damp straw. Old wood

smells. He saw the open front door, and beyond it a farmhouse. He wanted badly to sink into the straw at the back of the barn. But he moved on, toward the house.

Another pain-fried twenty yards, and he'd reached the small house. A door stood open. A man lay asleep on a sagging sofa in the front room; a radio crackled randomly on a lamp table beside him. An empty whiskey bottle lay on the rug beneath the snoring man. He was a middle-aged man in coveralls. That was all Milner noticed. He hobbled to him and tugged on his arm. "Hey, mister!" No response. He tried again and again but couldn't wake him. He looked around for a phone and couldn't find one. But there was a pickup truck out in the gravel drive. And a set of keys in the man's pocket.

Three minutes later, his face creased with pain, Milner was barreling the beat-up Ford pickup down the gravel road.

Ortega and Gordon watched him go, sagging against the porch railing of the farmhouse. Gordon said, "Shit."

Ortega nodded.

"We can't tell 'em he got away.... Anyway he'll be too scared to talk."

"I don't know," Ortega muttered. He glanced in the door of the house, saw the sleeping man and the whiskey bottle. He saw the empty one—and then spotted an unopened one, Old Crow, on a shelf over the refrigerator, which was at one end of the front room, beside a gas stove. The place had no kitchen.

"Not a complete waste," said Gordon, following Ortega's gaze.

The whiskey bottle in hand, they trudged off back by the barn—and stopped by the open door, hearing a woman giggle.

They looked at each other.

They listened.

They heard a man whispering huskily, and the girl giggling again. They went inside, and looking up at the loft, saw what Milner had missed: the straw moving as two people humped heartily away beneath it.

"What you think?" Gordon asked. "That the farmer's daughter or his wife?"

Ortega snorted and moved toward the ladder, unsheathing his knife. He stuck the knife in his teeth and started to climb.

"No, it don't have to be a complete waste," Gordon said, to no one in particular, following Ortega up the ladder.

The girl's screams didn't wake her snoring father.

6

The Wolf in His Den

Sullivan and Knickian were at a lunch counter at two the following afternoon; they were sorting again through the files on Swenson and his cronies, hoping for a hint in the killers' behavior pattern that would tell them where Swenson might have chosen to hide out. But Sullivan, sipping coffee gone tepid, was beginning to believe that this line of inquiry was a wild-goose chase. The KGB brains who were manipulating the goons had probably decided on the kidnappers' hiding place for them.

Frustrated, Sullivan looked up absently at a mini-TV on the chrome top of the soda fountain behind the gum-chewing waitress who was wiping down the counter. A news commentator was saying in a low tinny voice Sullivan could just make out, ". . . the killings were done in an identical style, involving a ritualistic cutting pattern which police believe is characteristic of certain types of lunatics who . . ."

Sullivan sat bolt upright. "Waitress! Do me a favor—turn up that news bulletin. Quick!"

She snorted, a little taken aback by the urgency in Sullivan's tone, but turned up the volume. Sullivan heard: "Police believe the killer or killers may still be in the Lightning Corners area."

Lightning Corners?

Sullivan bent over the sheaf of papers on the counter.

"What's the story, Sullivan?" Knickian asked, looking over his shoulder.

Sullivan found the page he was looking for. "Here—the bit about this guy Bloodsucker Gordon. He killed his victims ritualistically, cutting patterns into them, then sucking the blood from the wounds."

"Yuck!" the waitress cried reproachfully, turning down the volume on the TV.

"Lemme see that," Knickian said. He scanned the paper. "And that's what the guy on the TV news said?

"That's what he said."

"But where the hell is Lightning Corners?"

"I'll tell you something, man," Sullivan said, getting off his stool. "I've got no idea. But I'll tell you something else: I'm gonna find out."

After checking out the big, flat-black GMC van to be sure it hadn't been tampered with, Sullivan drove it out of the storage garage and over to his hotel. He parked across the street from the hotel—he'd left the penthouse for the time being, now that the KGB knew about it—and climbed into the van's back. He pulled the curtains that screened the rear from anyone looking in the front window; the rear windows were polarized. He could see out, but no one could see in. He bent over a rug on the floor and peeled it back. Beneath, in a coffin-sized compartment hidden beside the gas tank, were a half-dozen rifles, two submachine guns, a crossbow with sniperscope, and a variety of explosives. The equipment was held firmly in place with clamps and foam-rubber moldings; the plastic explosives in particular were carefully stored.

It was a highly illegal stash.

Sullivan selected a Heckler & Koch assault rifle, a

Browning Long Range Special with silencer attachment and sniperscope, the crossbow, and a Skorpion submachine gun. He took each weapon apart, cleaned and oiled it, inspecting the working parts for hairline cracks or jamming potential. He worked over the weapons methodically, expressionless. But it gave him a certain satisfaction. There was a keening anger in him, bottled up like a genie throwing a tantrum. He couldn't get his hands on the enemy just now, but preparing the killing tools was a step toward the vengeance-fulfillment he ached for.

Reading the Bremmer housekeeper's report on the cool, casual butchery of the two children as the kidnappers took their victims; seeing the quiet, incandescent pain in Celia Bremmer's eyes—these things brought about the familiar psychological shift in him. He'd become one with Celia Bremmer's anger at the senseless victimizing of her loved ones. He'd become one with her desire for vengeance. He knew, with a radiant inner certainty, that his enemy waited for him. He would not rest until that enemy was eradicated, erased, blotted out. Executed.

That's just the way he was.

Sullivan hastily zipped up his canvas bag and looked around the hotel room once more. No, nothing else. He was ready to seek out the killing ground. He went to the door, put his hand on the knob . . .

The phone rang.

He went to the table beside the bed and picked up the phone. "Yeah?"

He heard traffic sounds that told him the caller was at a pay phone. "Sullivan? Knickian. Listen, I'm being followed. But I gotta go back to my hotel room. Some papers there I need. The files. Can you meet me there, back me up?"

"You got it. But maybe you ought to wait where you are till I—"

But Knickian had hung up.

Sullivan replaced the earpiece and went grimly to the door. He had a bad feeling about this. Knickian should have waited.

He wished now he'd parked farther from the hotel. He might have been followed too.

He found a hallway window that opened onto a fire escape, and climbed through. He blinked in the sudden afternoon sunlight, then hurried down the fire escape stairs. He dropped to the sidewalk around the corner from the front entrance to the hotel, then doubled back, circling the block once before approaching the van. He saw no one stationed near the hotel, no one watching it. They might be in a building across the street, using surveillance equipment through a window. Or he might have successfully lost them when he went on his roundabout tail-eluding route after leaving his penthouse.

He unlocked the van, climbed up, and ten minutes later was only five blocks down the street and realizing his mistake. It was rush hour. He should have taken the subway. Because something told him he'd better get there quick. Come on you sons of bitches! he thought, honking, trying to work his way through a grid-locked intersection.

"Fuck it," he muttered, and drove the van up on the sidewalk. Honking wildly to make the pedestrians scatter for safety, he drove down the sidewalk, up one-way streets the wrong way, when they were clearer, and through red lights.

Knickian was staying in a broken-down hotel on Lexington. An obstacle course of hookers had to be run before you could get to the front door. They were all colors and shapes, including transsexuals with awkwardly built-up cheeks and knobby knees. Sullivan parked the van and jumped out, jogged toward the front door.

"Hey wanna date honey?"

"Hey sugar wanna go out?"

"Ooh he's *big!*"

Sullivan strode through them like they weren't there,

pushed through the double doors, and made a beeline across the grimy rug for the elevators. Room 312. Third floor. Maybe he should go up the stairs . . .

Someone bulky interposed himself between Sullivan and the door. "Hey, all visitors gotta check at the desk."

Sullivan literally walked right over the man.

The guy tried to put up a hand to stop him, and Sullivan walked into him and kept going as if the bouncer was just another swinging door. The guy stumbled back, fell, and Sullivan stepped on his chest and strode over him to the just-opening elevator. He could have easily avoided stepping on the guy without slowing, of course, but he stepped on him as a message: *Don't fuck with me.*

The guy didn't.

Sullivan stepped into the elevator and waited impatiently as it rattled lazily up two floors. On the way he hauled out the big Colt and checked to make sure it was loaded.

The elevator doors opened and he stepped out into the hall—the hackles on his neck rising. He had that bad feeling again. . . .

No one in the hall. He kept on, found room 312; it was locked.

"Knickian?" he shouted.

No reply.

He stepped back and kicked, gauging the kick perfectly: the door popped cleanly open and swung inward.

He slipped to one side, half-expecting gunfire from the room. Silence. He squatted low and peered around the corner of the door.

Knickian was there.

Sullivan stood and went in.

No one visible but Knickian. And Knickian was hanging from a cheap chandelier, a wire noose around his neck, his broken-nailed fingers frozen where they'd clawed at the wire, his face bloated and purple, tongue distended.

There was a note on the bed. Sullivan didn't more than glance at it. It was like he'd thought. A suicide note. A phony suicide note.

Sullivan looked toward the bathroom. The door was closed. He thought he heard a faint scraping sound from there.

The killer was still here. Hiding in the bathroom, thinking *cops*.

Partly to cut Knickian down—he'd liked the man, and he couldn't stand to see him hanging there like that, like a dead game bird on a wall peg—and partly to smoke out the killer, Sullivan fired the Colt at the wire suspending Knickian from the ceiling. The slug cut neatly through and the body fell like a sack of potatoes.

A bullet hole appeared in the bathroom door, and another. Judging by the high-pitched sound of the gunshot, the killer was toting a .32. The guy thought Sullivan's shot had been for him.

Sullivan had moved clear of the bathroom door. He was flattened against the wall beside it.

"Shit, you son of a bitch!" Sullivan gasped in his best imitation of a dying man. "You've shot off my fucking balls!"

The door creaked open. A hand with a gun emerged.

Sullivan fired from near-point-blank range, two shots in quick succession, and shot that hand right off its wrist. The gun went flying, and the hand hung for a moment from shreds, swinging, wrist spurting red.

Then the killer screamed and drew it back in. Sullivan swung to face the door to administer the coup de grace . . .

A hand grenade flung out the bathroom door came wobbling through the air at him.

Sullivan hadn't been expecting that. Not at all.

"Christ!" he blurted, slapping the grenade up and over his shoulder. He threw himself down and rolled under the bed as the grenade exploded near the ceiling.

The room shuddered; the windows spewed themselves tinkling onto the street; the chandelier crashed into a corner; chunks of ceiling fell and a bureau was flung onto its side. The room was choked with smoke and dust; Sullivan made out the shadowy shape of the assassin running from the bathroom to the open hallway door. He could see him holding his shattered hand to his belly, heard him sobbing with pain.

Coughing from smoke, Sullivan edged out from under the bed and got to his feet, following.

"Forget it!" Sullivan shouted. "You're not gonna make it! He was a friend of mine!" Sullivan was shouting in rage, not thinking about what was coming out at all. *"The Specialist is gonna nail your ass to the wall, motherfucker!"*

Sullivan had lost one too many friends recently.

The elevator doors closed in his face. The bastard was on his way down. Sullivan ran down the hall, figuring which room would be the right one. He'd noted a fire escape down the front of the building.

There, 317, facing the front. He tried the door. Locked. He smashed his shoulder against it; it splintered and gave, creaking inward.

A potbellied insurance salesman with a crooked toupee was humping a sag-titted whore on the box spring to the right; ahead was the window with the fire escape. It was painted shut.

The john saw Sullivan.

"My God!" the insurance salesman shouted, blanching, his erection wilting.

"Hey, Rex paid off the precinct bagman this morning, so what's the big idea?" the whore cawed, outraged.

Sullivan ignored them. He picked up a chair from beside the makeup table, dumped the clothes slung over it onto the floor, and flung it through the window. The glass shattered merrily, and two seconds later he followed the chair onto the fire-escape landing, then went banging down the black-painted metal steps.

He had reasons for not taking the regular stairs. There might already be cops in the lobby after that explosion. And he thought he might just drop in on the killer from an unexpected angle this way.

He reached the bottom landing and saw the KGB man from above. The killer was clutching his hand to his gut and mewling, climbing into the back of a small blue sedan just twenty feet below him. The car swung out from the curb.

Sullivan said, "Fuck it!"

He stuck the pistol in his rib holster, stepped up onto the metal railing, and jumped.

Sullivan was a big man, and no flying squirrel. But he worked out hard every day, and now he used his spring-steel leg muscles to propel him across the inter-vening space onto the trunk of the sedan, coming down hard enough to dent it badly in two places, wincing as slivers of pain shot up his ankles. He jounced, and nearly lost his balance, his arms wind-milling as the car lurched under him. He grabbed onto the roof, pulled himself farther up onto it, and held on.

The car veered frantically through the traffic, trying to dislodge him. He had a kaleidoscopic impression of cars flashing by, startled faces gaping at him from side windows, people on the street pointing. The wind squashed a bug on his chin and made his eyes water. He held on bitterly, fingers aching.

A police siren yowled behind them. Others would converge soon, and they might be as dangerous to Sullivan as to the KGB assassins in the car.

Apparently there were only two of them, because no one tried to roll down a window to get at him. The driver was preoccupied with dodging the cops despite the heavy traffic, and the guy in the back was proba-bly unconscious from blood loss by now.

The car arced sharply onto a near-empty side street; the sudden turn tore Sullivan from his hold and he went spinning sideways off the roof, falling onto the pavement. He struck flat on his back and felt like he'd been caught between a hammer and an anvil, all the wind knocked out of him. He lay stunned for a moment, trying to breathe. Something told him to open his eyes and move. Something: the sound of the blue sedan making a U-turn, coming back to run him down.

He gasped and got to his knees, fighting dizziness, and ripped his Colt from its holster, leveled it at the onrushing grille of the car. The grille was like the bared teeth of an animal, getting bigger and bigger. He knew how a mouse felt trying to stare down a cat.

He acted without thinking. The Colt bucked in his hand, twice. If mice carried .357 Colt revolvers, there'd be a lot more mice and a lot fewer cats in the world.

The right-front tire exploded, and the car careened out of control. It swerved, missing Sullivan by inches, and plowed into the rear of a parked garbage truck. It was one of those big rivet-heavy trucks with an immense garbage compressor like the oversized mouth of a bulldog; it was half-filled with garbage and beginning to compress. The sanitation workers had run for cover. Sullivan stood and shot out the rear window of the car, blasting the skull of the assassin in the back into cookie-sized chunks that went flying every which way in a bloody fireworks. The driver had jumped out and was lurching toward the sidewalk. Sullivan holstered the gun and, grinning, sprinted after him.

One part of his mind said: Take him and interrogate him. Don't kill him. He's useful.

But the rage was boiling over. And he seemed to see Knickian hanging from that cheap chandelier. . . .

He caught the gasping hit man by the neck and one leg, and in a rush of the superhuman strength that often came to him when the rage boiled up, he lifted him over his head and pitched him into the narrow gap in the closing garbage compactor.

The assassin screamed, and then the scream was cut off as the steel jaws pulped him like a squeezed tomato, merging his guts with filth.

They were just a half-block from the Soviet embassy; most of the garbage in the compactor was from there.

"Poetic justice, you son of a bitch," Sullivan remarked as the police cars began tearing down the street.

The police? There was no time to explain to the police. He had work to do.

He ran to the cab of the garbage truck and climbed up and threw the idling engine into gear.

Two police cars blocked his way, end to end across the street. He accelerated as much as he could, honking, and plowed through them where they met end-on, knocking them aside with a crashing peal of tortured metal. Those garbage trucks are *big*.

The cops were outside their cars, guns aimed over the trunks. Bullets whanged harmlessly from the steel hide of the big truck as Sullivan turned the corner. He pulled up beside a subway entrance, and praying for luck, jumped out of the truck and ran down the steps, vaulting the turnstile. Luck was there. The subway train was just leaving. He leapt onto the rear gate and climbed aboard. He rode a ways downtown, got out, and ran a few blocks to his van. It was undisturbed.

He climbed into the van, twisted the key in the ignition, threw it into gear, ripped out into the street, and burned rubber. No cops in sight—he'd given them the slip in the subway.

As he paused for traffic at a corner a few blocks on, he saw a newsboy waving a paper with the blunt black headline:

> KIDNAPPERS: "PAY
> NOW OR THEY DIE!"

There wasn't much time left.

He checked a New York State roadmap and found Lightning Corners—on the coast, upstate.

He put the map away and went to the nearest on-ramp for a freeway heading north.

And he was three miles out on the freeway before he realized that he was soaked in sweat and that his hands were shaking.

7

When They Come Like Locusts

The truck had run out of gas a mile back.

Milner had slept in a disused chicken coop on a heap of empty grain sacks. He'd done all the improvised medico work he could on his leg. The bullet had missed the artery and the major veins. The bleeding had stopped. Milner had stolen vegetables from a garden between the chicken coop and a ranch-style house, and he'd forced himself to eat a few raw.

He'd lain all night and most of the day in a feverish stupor, listening to the pitter-patter of mice and the distant calling of roosters as he drifted in and out of delirium.

He woke now, shivering in the late afternoon. He felt weak and vaguely disoriented. The pain in his leg was a throb that erupted into lancing fire when he moved.

Wincing, he sat up, took a few deep breaths, then pulled himself to his feet.

His stomach contracted and the world did a quick pirouette. The spinning slowed, stopped, and he knew he'd be okay for a while. Not long, though. He'd had gunshot wounds before, and he knew.

"Shit goddammit," he said between grinding teeth as he hobbled toward the door. "Shit. Shut up, leg. I know you've got a bullet in you, and I won't forget. I'll fix it, all right? Just quit reminding me about it. Stop nagging me, for God's sake."

He stood in the door of the chicken coop and looked around.

There was a burnt-sienna-colored ranch-style house, built as part of a housing development in 1970. Like all such houses, it was the same as the one next door except for being its mirror opposite. And like all such houses, it was badly built; the shingles were patched, the siding was coming loose, and there were big cracks in the concrete foundations, testifying to illegally cheap building materials. But the yard was neatly kept up. There was a moat of small white flowers around the house, and a white gravel path to the vegetable garden. A husky chained to the metal pole of the clothes-drying line ran in excited circles on a path it had worn in the grass, yipping when it saw Milner shambling toward the house.

Milner wasn't quite sure what to do.

If he asked for help, he'd be sent to a hospital. He'd have to explain the wound. The cops would come around, wondering how he'd gotten a wound like that—clearly from a military gun, as they'd see from the slug when the surgeon dug it out. He couldn't tell them about Martindale. The whole thing would come out then and he'd go to prison for years. They might execute him. Like the Rosenbergs. He'd been thinking of getting to a higher KGB functionary, denouncing Martindale, telling them Martindale and maybe Polonov were going to keep the money. But how to get to them? Martindale and McCarter had been his contacts. McCarter worked closely with Martindale, and however reluctantly, he'd approved the kidnapping. He might side with Martindale.

Get the leg fixed first, the pain told him.

A woman came out the back door of the garage, a bundle of wet laundry in her arms.

She scowled, seeing Milner. He realized that after spending a night running and sleeping in a chicken coop that he must look like a tramp.

She was white-haired, with wing-tip glasses and a leathery, lined face.

"I'm sorry to bother you, lady . . . I just want to ask where there's a doctor. And where I am. I . . . got lost in the woods. Hurt my leg. I've got some money, though. I'm . . . not a bum." He reached into his back pocket. The wallet was gone. Ortega must have taken it while he was stunned.

"Lost that too I guess," he said sheepishly.

"Get out of here. My husband will be back in five minutes," she said in a voice like two wires scraping.

"Lady, I need a doctor. I'm really not a bum."

She cocked her head at him. "Up the road east about a quarter-mile. Says Golding on the mailbox. He's a doctor. Might be home. And where this is, it's just outside Lightning Corners."

"Oh. Of course. Thank you. I'll uh . . . ." He peered past her into the garage. It was empty. "Mind if I pass through the garage to the road?"

She said nothing, but stepped back out of his way.

He walked past her, through the late-afternoon sunshine, and into the cool shadow of the garage. It smelled like damp concrete and oil. He glanced over his shoulder. She was standing in the doorway, outlined in sun glare, the clothes still bunched in her arms like a big cloth cabbage. She was watching him go.

He kept going, out onto the drive. He glanced back again. She had gone to hang up the wet clothes. He returned to the garage, trying to make no noise. He'd seen two things there he needed. One was a bottle of Coca-Cola in a crate of pop bottles in the corner. He slipped it out.

The other thing he needed was a knife. He'd seen a hunting knife hanging in a rack of tools over a wooden bench to one side. He took it, and felt a little better.

Ortega and Gordon might be driving around looking for him. The knife wasn't much defense against their guns, but it was better than nothing.

He slipped the knife into his khaki shirt and tucked it, in its leather sheath, in his waistband.

Then he hobbled back out onto the road. The sun was hot on the back of his neck. The Coca-Cola was twist-top, and he drank it gratefully, though it was warm. It gave him a slight lift. He hurried on, as much as he could hurry; after a while he felt a warm trickling at the back of his leg. The wound had opened again. His stomach burned from the acidic soft drink.

He was trudging along a sun-softened strip of asphalt. Grass-lined ditches to either side ran with thin streams of rainwater, left over from the day before. He passed between a succession of nearly identical houses, feeling like he was on some kind of infinite treadmill, that he was not going anywhere, that he'd died and gone to hell. His leg itched and stung and his head ached. His muscles complained with cramps about the hours spent on the feedsacks.

After what seemed an endless effort, he saw a mailbox that said "G.B. GOLDING, M.D." There was a tan VW Bug in the driveway.

He turned in at the drive. There were voices from around back. He turned the corner and walked along a strip of grass between two nearly alike houses, grateful for the momentary shade.

A startled gasp made him look up. A man with car keys in his hand was staring at him. Probably en route from the backyard to the car. He was a young man with shiny black hair and yellow-tinted glasses, a weak chin.

"You Golding?" Milner asked him.

The man nodded.

"You're a doctor, right? I need one. I've had an accident. A kid playing around with a gun . . . uh, target shooting. Shot me in the leg."

Golding looked at him and at his clothes, and clearly didn't believe him. Milner realized his fatigues and khaki might look institutional—like some kind of prison uniform. Maybe Golding was taking him for an escaped prisoner. He'd call the cops.

He was only two paces away.

Milner said, "I've got some identification . . ." He reached into his shirt, stepped toward the smaller man—and pulled out the knife, unsheathing it in a second, pressing it to the doctor's neck. "Listen," Milner whispered. "I haven't done anything wrong. I've been trying to help this country. But someone tried to kill me and they chased me through the woods and I'm hurt bad and I'm afraid I've got to be tough with you. Now, take me to where you've got some medical supplies, and hurry."

Golding swallowed, making his Adam's apple jog against the knife blade. That made him wince. "Sure thing. Around the front."

Milner nodded and stepped behind him. He held the knife flat against Golding's throat, and the two walked awkwardly around to the front. Golding opened the door and they went in. Milner hoped no one had seen them.

He was feeling dizzy.

"Now, don't fuck around, doc, because I was in Nam and I had a lot of wounds and I know how it works. So no cute injections, okay?"

"Sure, sure. Right in here."

They went into a bedroom that had been converted into an office.

Milner could hear laughing voices out back. A few neighbors over for beer maybe. Probably the doc had been going out for more. Good thing no one was indoors.

Milner lay on the examination table, on his side. "Come around to my front, with your bag and stuff, where I can reach you with the knife if you get ideas—"

"I won't, mister. Listen, why don't you—?"

"No. Shut up and do it." The doctor took a black bag from a shelf and came around to Milner's front.

"Okay," Milner said. "Now, uh . . . just cut open

the cloth and do the work. Spritz some local anaes-
thetic on it. I'll have to do without any stronger."

The doctor did as he was told and it hurt like a son
of a bitch.

After the wound was bandaged, Milner took some
vitamins, a handful of codeine, and a two-day-old
roast-beef sandwich.

He tied the doctor up in the kitchen and took ten
dollars from his wallet.

"See? I'm taking ten dollars. I'm not a thief—I could
take the whole forty you've got there."

Golding just stared at him, shaking ever so slightly,
his eyes going now and then to the knife.

Voices at the back door. Two men coming in the
house. Two late for hostages.

He took the car keys and the sandwich and limped
out the front door. He got into the VW, started it, and
put it into gear. He heard shouting behind him.

The car lurched forward and he sped off down the
street toward Lightning Corners.

He felt a combination of elation and dread. At least
he'd gotten the bullet out. Things would be better. He'd
find his way back to Manhattan.

But the worst was yet to come.

Dr. Golding's friends were untying him and asking
questions. Golding, who'd always had a fascination
with slashers, owing to certain sick fantasies of his
own, said, "That slasher, the guy who cut up that
couple in the barn across the hollow—I think that was
him! He had a knife and this crazy look! And he took
my car!"

He ran to the telephone.

Sullivan sat in his flat-black van across from the
sheriff's office in Lightning Corners and wondered
where to start. Swenson and the other kidnappers had
to be in this area somewhere because that killing, the
butchery of the two young lovers in a farmer's barn,

was precisely Bloodsucker Gordon's style of killing. And that had happened only a mile from here.

Sullivan was trying to think up a pretense for asking directions to the scene of the murder, wondering what he could safely get out of the cops.

Maybe he could pass himself off as a private eye. No. No way. Maybe . . .

A surge of mass movement, seen from the corner of his eye, made him look out the side window.

A mob had formed in the street of this sleepy hamlet, and it looked very much out of place.

"What the hell . . ." Sullivan breathed.

Thirty men and about ten teenage boys, plus a few women, were surging around a tan VW Bug on the next corner to Sullivan's rear. Even from here he could see red faces, angry eyes, mouths open to shout. They were rocking the VW between them, threatening to overturn it. One of them had blocked its forward path with a Chevy pickup. As Sullivan watched, the VW's rear was blocked by a station wagon. He couldn't see who was inside it.

Someone with a shotgun blew out the car's tires, one by one, methodically. The crowd cheered.

Acting on a hunch, Sullivan got out of the van, locked it, and crossed the street to a group of the more passive locals, watching with wide eyes and gaping mouths.

"Hi," Sullivan said, doing his best to be charming. "One of you mind telling me what's going on over there?"

A tall pop-eyed man with a sunburned bald spot said, "What I heard, they think they got the slasher. The guy that cut those kids to pieces. This guy had a bullet in his leg, what I heard, and he went to Dr. Golding, used a big knife to force him to fix the leg up, and then he woulda slashed him up, but the doc's friends all came in. So the guy took off in the doc's car. That's his car for sure. So the doc called the cops, and the family of one of those kids, the Windemeres, they were in the sheriff's office and heard the call coming in, and the sheriff went out looking for the guy, but he went in the wrong direction—which is typical—and right away down the street comes the Doc's Bug, probably 'cause you got to go through town to get to the freeway. So the Windemeres spotted that car and knew it for sure and they—"

"But there must be lots of VW bugs like that," Sullivan objected.

"It's got his kids' baby shoes in the window. We all know it. So anyway, see, Windemere went to the grange hall where they was right then having a farmers' meeting about the rise in criminality around here. Windemere got 'em out on the streets."

"I just can't figure this kind of mob action around here," said one of the other men.

"Well, it's like this," said the pop-eyed guy, who was evidently the local sage, "we got us two communities here. The farmers' community, and the people who moved here from the city. They're commuters or retirees and they don't give a damn about this stuff. They're the majority. But the farmers, they knew those kids, and those kids were both loved hereabouts, that girl was the homecoming queen. And there's been all this talk about how the courts put a fellow in jail and then let him out a few years later and he goes out and does the same thing again, especially these psychos, and people are pissed off about that."

Sullivan nodded. He could sympathize. But there was still too much chance the mob had the wrong man. And his instinct for detecting evil in men told him that the man they had was innocent, when— after smashing the car's windows and unlocking the doors—they dragged him out of the car and down the street.

Sullivan looked at the man and didn't sense the kind of evil that would make a psycho killer.

Some called it a psychic ability, others said it was simply concentrated observation, the ability to see into a man from the look of him. Whatever it was, Jack Sullivan had a talent: he knew when a man was guilty; when the enemy—the free-floating evil that lived in the world—had taken him. He had always had the talent, and he'd never been wrong on the question of guilt. In this respect there was perhaps no one else on the face of the earth like him.

A moment later, as the crowd dragged the terrified, blinking man nearer, Sullivan recognized him. It was Milner. He knew him from the file photographs.

They were dragging him to a car that was waiting at the corner, more convenient for quick exits than the pickup or the station wagon. Looked as if they planned to take him out into the country and execute him.

Sullivan made up his mind.

He needed Milner alive. If the cops got him, Sullivan probably wouldn't have access to him. If the mob killed him, that would dry up one of his leads. He sighed. It would be difficult to extricate Milner from the mob without hurting any of them.

He decided he could allow himself to break a few bones if he had to.

The crowd had jammed Milner into the car—an old yellow Impala—and Sullivan, getting as near as he could, heard the driver say, "Singer Point!"

The men he spoke to nodded and led the rest of the crowd off toward the pickup and station wagon.

The yellow Impala burned rubber and broke the speed limit, heading east toward the sea.

Sullivan unlocked the van and climbed in. He checked his map, running his callused forefinger down the coastline. He found Singer Point, near the swampy Singer Beach Bird Sanctuary, and worked out the route. Then he started the van and stepped on the gas. Behind him a leather-clad figure on a motorcycle tightened a helmet strap, gunned the motorcycle, and took off in pursuit.

* * *

The men in the car were talking, but Milner wasn't aware of what they were talking about. He wasn't listening.

He was somewhere else, mentally. He'd retreated into delirium.

In his head he was back in Nam, chained to a bracket in a Soviet-built armored car bumping up a jungle trail through the sticky air and the burdensome heat, one of five prisoners being taken to a "special" camp. He expected special torture at the special camp. But once he got there, no one laid a hand on him. He was amazed. They smiled at him, fed him well, and behaved as if he were a confused child who needed their patience. They never hit him, or cut him. But the Sessions—those were hard in another way. Dr. Chih would give him the autohypnotic drug and begin the lessons. He would show him photos of the massacre at My Lai and other atrocities perpetrated by the Americans. They didn't discuss the Vietcong's own acts of atrocity. Chih talked of the poverty in the world, and played again and again on the fact that Milner, then Benson—Benson was his real name—had come from an upper-middle-class background. It was very easy for Comrade Benson to be bland about the starving poor, to say that the world inevitably had a percentage of such people and one man could not cure all the world's ills—such problems had never touched Comrade Benson because he had been a member of the privileged elite. And so Chih worked at Milner's already developed guilt complex, turning the young lieutenant's mind into a snake pit of self-doubts.

Two years later, Milner was converted.

Now, the way a dying man will see his life pass before him, Milner was reliving his brainwashing, his Marxist indoctrination, the turning, his assignment to Soviet authorities, his new identity and his new philosophy. He had been made over. He had even thought of himself as "Milner" and not Benson.

But now . . . Now, as the delirium passed. . . .

The web of deceit and suggestion Chih had worked into his mind was collapsing under the weight of trauma. He was becoming himself again, at least philosophically. He still thought of himself as Milner, after years of habit. But the deeper self had resurrected. He was from this moment on no longer a Marxist. He was an American, a believer in free enterprise, and a soldier in the U.S. Army.

He opened his eyes, and remembered where he was. In a car with six grim men who planned to kill him. And they *would* kill him. Two of them were carrying guns, and they had taken away his knife. They'd never listen to him.

They'd kill him for sure, and he'd die unredeemed, with the world thinking he was not only a traitor to his country—the thought brought a lump to his throat— but also a sex killer.

"You know something?" said the driver, peering in the rearview mirror. "I think somebody's following us. Somebody who's not supposed to be—he's making the same turns. Any of you guys know that black van?"

8

The Professional and the Amateurs

Bremmer was trying not to listen to them. He had to keep sane, and calm, and not let them get to him. But they weren't talking directly to him or his daughter now. The loonies were talking among themselves, on the floor near the bed where his daughter was tied up. They made plans, and Bremmer knew that if they were making plans where he could hear them, then they definitely planned to kill him and June, ransom or no ransom.

Swenson sat with his back to the wall, as he always did. He had the lantern between his legs, illuminating him eerily from beneath. Esmeralda sat to his right, Gordon and Ortega across from him. Gordon was gaping, looking like a kid watching a war movie with great pleasure, as Swenson droned on about his hell vision.

"Once we get the money, we'll have to eliminate those Russian goons. You know that, of course. We don't want pig Soviets in charge any more than we want pig Americans. Then we'll take the money—"

"But the KGB," said Ortega, who spoke only when it was about a practical matter, "will come after us."

"We'll keep clear of them. They don't have the run of this country. It's not like they're the Mafia," Swenson said. "And anyway, we've got to erase our Martindale and Polonov and Garcia." He spoke in whispers now. "Because they're planning to kill *us* soon. I can feel it."

Esmeralda nodded as if she'd just had a confirmation from the spirit world. "I have *seen* it. They'd like to kill us."

"We will kill them, and we will play with our little friends here, the way we ought to be able to"—he indicated Bremmer and his daughter—"and then we'll bury them, and we'll take the money and we'll build with it. We'll buy a small army of mercenaries, the kind who don't care as long as they're paid, and we'll use them to break into the shitholes where they kept the Righteous"—meaning the asylums—"and we'll free our brothers and sisters, and we'll make a great army, and we'll take it to a southern place, maybe New Mexico . . ."

Esmeralda gasped. "Yes! New Mexico! The spirits of the dark world are strong there!"

"And we'll make a home, and prepare, and we'll kill anyone among us who is not of the Hidden Race of Vision, and we will know them by signs from the Dark Places, and we will hunt out those in the towns around our little fetus nation, and we will kill those who are our natural enemies, we will kill and feed—"

"Feed!" said Bloodsucker Gordon delightedly.

"—feed on their blood and souls and grow stronger like the African who eats the heart of his enemy to grow strong, and we will eat the heart of the world and have all the power in the world, and we will kill . . ."

Bremmer tried not to listen as Death continued to whisper its plans for him and the world.

It was nearly seven when the yellow Impala turned onto the Singer Beach access road.

Sullivan followed and made his assessment: this

was the place. It was secluded enough, and there wasn't much time left.

The van—which Knickian had called the Vangeance—was supercharged, with an unusually large engine for a van, V-8, and four-wheel-drive. Still, it wasn't unusually fast—for the simple reason that it was so heavily armored.

It didn't *look* armored. From the outside it seemed a normal GMC van. But it was steel-reinforced inside, with armoring customized to Sullivan's specifications. There were camouflaged firing slits in the doors and sides. The windows were bullet-proof and the underside specially proofed against fire and explosives.

He glanced in his rearview mirror. The pickup and the station wagon were still nowhere in sight. They were probably at least a mile behind. But there was someone in black leather on a motorcycle. One of those sinister-looking opaque helmets.

He shrugged. Probably just a joyrider.

He turned his attention to the Impala.

The road was curving south to follow the coastline. On the right were the marshlands and estuaries of the Singer Bird Sanctuary; beyond, the red-gold sun was resting on the tops of the trees, preparing to dive into sunset. To the left, down a short precipice of perhaps ten feet, was a sandy gray beach flecked with boulders. The sea rolled in and out along the scallops of the beach.

The Impala was about fifty yards ahead. Then forty-five, forty, thirty-five yards, as Sullivan accelerated.

The van had other features Sullivan was sorry he couldn't use in this case. It would have simplified things to use the rocket launcher concealed in the blunt nose of the van—it was built to look like part of the underpinning of the dashboard. Also under a dashboard concealment panel was a radarscope, not unlike the sort police use to come down on speeders. The radar gave Sullivan the exact distance of the target; the rocket obliterated the target. So far he hadn't had the chance to use it, except in tests. This equipment too was highly illegal.

Thirty yards to the Impala, twenty-five, twenty . . .

The sun began to slide below the treetops; long shadows like the fingers of night itself began to reach across the road to the ocean. As the dark fingers fell over the sedan, Sullivan moved in.

An eighth-mile up ahead was a soft, sandy road shoulder contained by a rim of sandy land over the beach. He accelerated, cut around to the sedan's right, riding the gravel edge of the road; he glimpsed startled faces in the car's windows, then jerked the steering wheel to the left, hard. His customized ramming bumper absorbed the impact without losing the push, and the yellow Impala squealed to the left, fishtailing as the driver fought for control. A window rolled down and a gun muzzle poked through and flashed. Buckshot whined harmlessly from the windows of the van, only slightly scoring the paint job on the side door with the second blast. Sullivan jerked the wheel over again, at the same time angling to avoid an outthrust of the marshland to his right. He slammed the van's bumper into the Impala's right front door, deeply denting it, sending up a shower of sparks. The Impala fishtailed again, this time going into the left lane. The gunman was trying to get a bead on Sullivan's tires. Sullivan didn't give him the chance. He slammed the Impala once more as it drew abreast of the road shoulder, and this time it careened out of control, sliding sideways to smack into the wall of sod and gravel.

"Dammit," Sullivan muttered as the car turned over. It was on its roof now, sliding down the bank to the beach, where it came to rest, rocking, windows broken out.

Sullivan pulled up sharply, straining against the wheel with the inertia. The motorcyclist coming up from behind looped around him, narrowly missing a collision with the van's rear end. Sullivan was preoccupied with a U-turn and didn't see the biker slow and circle back.

He parked on the little bluff over the place where the Impala had gone down, and, worried that he'd find the occupants of the car dead, he unholstered his Colt and climbed out.

He ran to a path circling the rim and skidded down it to the beach, coming up behind the overturned car. Its wheels spun, slowing. It looked like a turtle on its back. One of the doors was hanging open, and a man lolled out, groaning.

Sullivan moved up cautiously and checked him over. Looked like he had a broken arm. Not much more, unless there were internal injuries.

Sullivan crouched, the Colt leveled, and found he was looking into the face of the man who'd held the shotgun. He was on the farther side, had worked himself around to upright. He swung the gun toward Sullivan.

"Uh-uh," Sullivan said, and shot it neatly from his hands.

The man yelped as the bullet smacked into the shotgun's breech, the impact sending tight shock waves to sting his hands. He dropped the gun and covered his eyes. "Don't shoot!"

"Milner," Sullivan shouted to the dazed, upside-down man in the confused tangle of limbs. "You okay? Can you climb out?"

Milner grunted and wormed his way free. The other men, seeing the Colt, made no move to stop him.

Sullivan looked over the driver, who appeared stunned, his nose broken. He didn't seem mortally hurt.

Milner and Sullivan backed away from the sedan, worked their way into the cover of a cluster of boulders, and climbed up to the road.

Milner was too dazed to ask questions.

The station wagon and the pickup, both crammed full with amateur vigilantes, were approaching as Milner and Sullivan climbed into the black van.

Sullivan leaned out his window and shouted as they went by, pointing to the beach. "Your friends are down there—they need help!"

The vigilantes probably hadn't heard him, but they saw the gesture and the skid marks, and no sign of their friends on the road, so they stopped. What they didn't see was Milner, who was hiding under Sullivan's dashboard, jammed down near the floor.

Sullivan gunned the van into life and shot it down the road, back the way he'd come. It was dusk now. He was distracted from noticing the single headlight in his rearview mirror by Milner, who finally managed to ask, "Who the hell are *you*?"

Sullivan snorted. "My name's Sullivan. I'm a friend or an enemy, depending on how you feel about cooperating with me."

"What kind of cooperating is that?" Milner asked, rubbing a bruise on his forehead. As a sort of afterthought, to himself, he added, "Man, I feel lousy. Leg's bleeding again."

Sullivan drove with one hand. The other was on the Colt, which he held, casually but in complete control, on his right thigh.

It was pointing nowhere in particular at the moment. Milner knew a pro when he saw one. He knew Sullivan could whip the gun barrel around and blow him away without taking his eyes off the road.

"What I want," said Sullivan, "is for you to talk, quick, about the location of Bremmer and his daughter, and the assholes who've got them."

9

The Unexpected Gun

Milner talked, all right. He talked, and he kept talking, and Sullivan listened. After a while Sullivan put away the gun.

His talent for judging people had come into play again. He knew that Milner was telling the truth—that Swenson and the others were truly Milner's enemies; that Milner had turned, again, and was now, for good, loyal to the American way of life.

"Communism is a lie," Milner said. "A beautiful lie. It would be so great if it could be true—a society in which everyone shares everything in which no one group of men controls the means of production, the resources, the big money, the land. . . . But it will always be that way: some men will struggle to win out over others, and whether it's in a socialist system or a capitalist system, it doesn't matter. People are the same everywhere—some few of them will gravitate into power and exploit the others. At least in a capitalist system everyone has a chance. I knew about the Soviet repression, of course, but I told myself it was a kind of . . . of evolutionary process, that the dictatorship there is temporary. But I see it now.

Chih lied to me. Martindale lied to me. There's no idealism in the Communist governments that exist. Because there's no democracy in them."

They sat in the dark cab of the van, the only light a ghostly green from the dashboard dials. They were parked in the back lot of a Mobil station that had gone out of business. Its windows were whitewashed, and some of the locals had begun using its broken-in garage as a trash dump. Now and then a car's lights searched along the highway on the other side of the deserted station and then slid into darkness.

Sullivan glanced at his watch: it was nearly one A.M. not yet time to case the farmhouse.

"What really hurts," Milner said, "is all the time I lost. And the damage I did. I mean, all those years. I cost the U.S. government millions of bucks. I . . ." His voice broke.

"You just might get a chance to make it up," Sullivan said, taking a whiskey flask from his glove compartment. They'd just eaten, from Sullivan's supplies. Sullivan liked a shot of whiskey or two after a meal. He was, after all, partly Irish.

He poured whiskey into two coffee cups and passed one to Milner, saying evenly, with not a bit of theatrics: "Here's to the death of this country's enemies."

"Here's to that," said Milner, and meant it.

They drank, and a shotgun blast smashed into the windshield from about ten feet away.

"Holy shit!" Milner shouted, ducking.

Sullivan had flinched but hadn't bothered ducking—he knew it would take more than a twelve-gauge shotgun to break those windshields.

The muzzle flash had come from an open doorway at the rear of the service station. Someone had come into the garage through the front, skirted the trash heap, and taken up a firing position just inside the back door.

Sullivan shrugged. It was time to take a chance on Milner. He reached under the seat and drew out a

Beretta automatic pistol. He slipped a clip into it and gave it to Milner, butt-first. "Here. Cover me. Through the slit in the sidewall."

Milner grunted and followed Sullivan into the rear of the van, as another shotgun blast boomed, singing off the metal of the side door.

"Sounds like the same gun. From the same place," Milner said. "Maybe only one person."

"Maybe." Sullivan unlocked the firing slot and pressed it aside. "Fire through here. Just try to keep 'em down."

Hunched over, he went to the back door, opened it, and slipped out into the night. From here he should be concealed from the unknown gunman in the garage by the bulk of the van.

He faded into the darkness, slipping into a stand of elms between the service station and a creek. He had the big .357 Colt in his hand as he moved through the trees, parallel to the creek, one hand feeling ahead to guard against snags from tree limbs. He came to a wooden fence, chest-high, and climbed over it, dropping to the asphalt road on the other side. He turned back toward the highway.

All the time he wondered if the sporadic gunfire from the van—the popping of the little Beretta and the occasional answering roar of the shotgun—would be heard at the farmhouse a quarter-mile down the road, where the kidnappers were hiding out. If they heard it, they might decide to pack up and move on.

He came around to the front of the service station and slipped into the garage, carefully stepping over the broken-down remnants of a garage door. A Honda 500, jet black and green-trimmed, was parked to one side, gleaming in the light from a passing car on the road. That same light swung for a moment like a prison searchlight over the interior of the garage, making shadows dance and picking out a skewed pyramid of trash sacks and beer cans, and, to the right of the heap, a leather-jacketed figure in a motorcycle helmet at the back door, reloading a shotgun.

In that brief flare of light Sullivan memorized the terrain. He crept across the concrete, stepped over a swollen plastic sack, the gun tilted slightly upward in his right hand.

The darkness returned, complete and odorous with garbage.

Sullivan misjudged a step—and rattled a tin can with his booted foot.

He heard the gunman whirl, and the sound of the shotgun being pumped as a round was cranked into its chamber.

Sullivan dropped to the floor, unwillingly embracing a ruptured trash sack as the shotgun thundered, lighting up the garage for an instant. He had a glimpse of a startling face under the open visor of a motorcycle helmet. The shot blasted harmlessly overhead.

As his assailant pumped another round into the chamber, Sullivan got to his knees and pitched the trash sack at the gunman. He was unwilling to use the Colt till he knew who he was shooting at.

The gunman grunted in surprise as the trash sack struck, and there was a clattering sound. A bullet whined off the concrete by Sullivan's right foot—a stray shot from the Beretta. "Hold your fire, Milner!" Sullivan shouted, and, holstering the Colt, he charged the shotgunner.

The gunman stepped back through the doorway and Sullivan saw the leather-jacketed figure, slender and black-clad, outlined against the star gleam on the shiny side of the van. Sullivan kept coming, and struck the stranger in the gut, so the motorcyclist folded around his fist, gagging, the shotgun falling to the pavement. Sullivan followed up with a left-handed karate chop to the neck, just beneath the helmet, paralyzing a key nerve. The stranger sagged.

Sullivan caught the slumping figure in his arms and carried him to the back of the van, thinking that the man was surprisingly lightweight. It must be that his flash impression in the garage was correct, this was just a young boy.

He laid the unknown gunman out on the rug in the back of the van and switched on an interior light. Then he reached out and unfastened the helmet, as Milner came limping around to look over his shoulder.

He pulled off the helmet, and grunted with surprise.

The gunman was beautiful.

She was perhaps twenty-one, with naturally copper-red hair full of waves that were almost curls; her face was pleasantly plump, ivory pale, with a delicate spray of freckles across the small, perfect nose. Her lips were bee-stung, her chin impishly pointed, and when her eyes opened, long dark red eyelashes fluttering, they flashed crystal blue.

"Christ!" Milner said. "He's a girl!"

She blinked, and looked back and forth between Sullivan and Milner. Sullivan's face made her freeze for a moment—it was scarred and hard-looking—and fear flickered in her blue eyes. But the fear quickly became anger. She kicked, catching Sullivan by surprise, her karate kick booting him in the gut. Now it was Sullivan's turn to double over and gasp. She aimed a second kick at Milner, but he'd backed away by then.

Sullivan, recovering but still red-faced, caught her kicking leg by the ankle and twisted it to force her over onto her belly.

"You bastards! You're not going to rape *me*!" she yelled.

As a matter of fact, Sullivan had been thinking what a lovely ass she had—it was well-defined by her tight black leather pants. But he had no intention of raping her; he believed in either castration or execution for rapists. Or both.

He reached out, grabbed one of her wrists, and twisted it behind her back, exerting enough pressure to make her groan.

"You quiet down and behave, and I'll let you loose," he said. "We've got no intention of raping you or hurting you. But we just might have to put you on ice for a while."

"Okay, okay . . ." she muttered.

He let go, and moved back out of kicking range.

She turned to face them, crouching, brushing her hair from her eyes with a black-gloved hand.

"What's the big idea with the shotgun?" Milner demanded.

She spat at him. "Murderer!"

Sullivan nodded. "I see. You think he did it too. You knew those kids who were murdered?"

She looked at him a little confusedly, less certain of herself now.

"Sure I knew them. She was my cousin and he was a friend of mine. I grew up with them." Tears formed in her eyes; she swallowed to hold back a sob.

"Uh-huh." Sullivan sat down across from her, his legs crossed Indian-style. "Listen to me . . ." He looked her in the eyes. "This man's name is Milner. He was mistakenly identified as the killer by a hysterical doctor who doesn't know shit about the case. The man who killed your friend and your cousin is probably a guy named Bloodsucker Gordon, part of the Swenson cult. You know who Swenson is?"

"Sure." Her eyes were wide now. "I heard he got out of the asylum. But that was on the West Coast."

"He had help, and the help brought him here. I'll tell you the whole story, if you want." He glanced at his watch. "We've got time. I want to wait till most of them are asleep before I look over the place."

"You know where they are?"

"Milner does." Sullivan grinned. "The guy you were trying to rub out was the only hope of finding the bastards who killed your cousin."

She looked at him, head cocked. "Maybe this is a lot of bullshit to cover up—"

He began, "Look—"

"You know, you look familiar," she said suddenly. "Hey, can I get something from the rack of my bike?"

"Another gun?"

"No. A magazine."

Sullivan shrugged. "Okay, we keep the shotgun. If

you come back shooting, you'll come up against the armor again and this time we'll run you down. Understand?"

"Sure."

"And if you run off to get your friends, we'll be gone when you come back."

"My friends? You mean that lynch mob?" She snorted in contempt. "That bunch of fuck-ups? They couldn't lynch a dead cow."

Sullivan chuckled, and decided against mentioning that she hadn't done very well at executing sentence on Milner herself.

"Where'd you learn martial arts?" he asked, rubbing his still-smarting belly.

"The Wacs. I'm a sergeant. I'm on leave. Can I get the magazine?"

"Magazine? Sure, go ahead," said Sullivan, puzzled. *Magazine?*

She went out between them, moving a little stiffly, as if she expected one of them to grab her.

When she'd gone, Milner said, "You sure that was a good idea, letting her go?"

"No. I'm not sure it was a good idea to trust you, either."

Milner had nothing to say to that.

She came back a minute later, her face rosy with excitement. "I was right!" She sat down beside Sullivan, her fear of him evidently vanished, and handed him a copy of *Soldier of Fortune* magazine, open to a double-page spread headed: "THE SPECIALIST"— WHO IS HE?

"Oh, no," said the Specialist.

On the right-hand page he saw an old photo of himself, in uniform, taken from Armed Services files. Beside it was a composite sketch of the Specialist, looking older and more grizzled, and scarred, the expression grim. Beneath the two pictures were the words: "Is this the same man?" He scanned the article. It was a roughly accurate rundown of his mercenary exploits, his now-legendary one-man war against Magg

Ottoowa, and a more accurate list of his accomplishments in Nam.

"It's you, isn't it?" she asked, tapping the picture of the smiling young man in the Special Forces uniform.

Sullivan shrugged. "Funny, I was just asking myself that. Seems like another guy now. But in the way you mean, yeah." He tossed the magazine aside. "Damn them. I'm going to cancel my subscription. I'll need plastic surgery."

"It says the cops are looking for you."

Sullivan smiled. "Not too hard, they're not."

Milner looked at the magazine and then at Sullivan, awed. "Damn, you said your name was Sullivan. And Martindale mentioned the Specialist—but I guess what with all that happened I was too dazed to make the connection."

Sullivan lit a Lucky Strike and climbed up to the driver's seat. Then he turned to the girl. "You know *my* name . . ."

"My name's Beth. Beth Pepper."

"Okay, Sergeant Pepper, listen: we're going to get the people that killed your cousin and your friend. So if you'll refrain from shooting at us and refrain from talking about me at all—anytime—we'll let you go."

"Let me *go*? Now that I've found you, I'll be darned if I'll . . ." Her face reddened. "What I mean is, I want to be in on it. Getting the guy who did that to Lois."

Sullivan groaned. "Not this again! Listen—"

"Are you going to be a male chauvinist and pretend I can't be of any use? I'm a Wac! Give me an M16 and I'll knock a tin can off a treetop at two hundred yards! And I nearly took *you* out with that karate kick, didn't I?"

Sullivan sighed. "Sure, okay, I guess I'm old-fashioned. But being as you're a Wac—"

"Sergeant Pepper!" Milner said, chuckling. The girl silenced him with a glare.

"—being as you're a Wac, you know something about military discipline. So you can take orders, right? And you know who's in command?"

"Sure, Captain!" she said, grinning.

"Okay. I figure to check out the farm and hit it just at dawn. I figure even their sentries will be bleary then. That gives us five hours—and we'd better get out of here before the local sheriff finally puts on his pants and gets out here. All that shooting, somebody probably called in."

She nodded. "I know just the place. I'm staying at my parents' place while I'm on leave. They're out of town now."

There was something about the way she was looking at him that made Sullivan nervous.

Normally he wouldn't have minded. Normally, in fact, he'd have dived right into it. But he was on the verge of a firefight and that was no time to be distracted by sex.

And Beth was looking at him like she wanted to eat him alive.

10

Ignoring the Good Advice of Indians

"And you say this guy Martindale is really a Soviet KGB agent?" Beth said, astonished at having stumbled onto so tangled a nest of snakes.

"That's right," Milner said a little weakly. Sullivan looked at him as they pulled up at Beth's house. Milner looked pale and shaky. He was still weak from blood loss.

"It's kind of late to eat," Sullivan said, "but I think our friend here ought to."

Milner looked at him gratefully—not because Sullivan suggested he should eat, but because Sullivan had called him "friend."

Beth said, "Sure, I can make steaks. And I'll give him some iron pills."

An hour later they sat around the checkered-cloth-covered kitchen table, all of them a little drowsy in the warmth from the rumbling gas heater in the corner and the big meal. Milner's meal in the van had been Spartan.

Milner was drooping in his chair.

"Go on, Milner, lie down somewhere," Sullivan said. "That's an order."

"There's a blanket on the couch," Beth said.

"Guess I . . . better rest," Milner managed, stumbling into the living room.

Beth said, "Well . . . you going to sleep?" She looked at Sullivan.

He shook his head. "I could use it. But I find if I sleep right before a dawn firefight, I'm more blurry than if I simply stay up all night."

"Okay. You want some speed?"

Sullivan scowled. "Where are you getting that? Prescription?"

"What? Uh . . . no. I just buy it from a guy at the base. He's got speed, acid, hash, cocaine—"

Sullivan's outburst of cursing cut her off. She looked at him, surprised. "I take it you don't approve."

"Approve? Of a guy selling drugs on a military base? Does he sell heroin?"

"Yes."

"Uh-huh. If I caught him at it, I'd strangle him on the spot."

She stared at him. "You really mean it, don't you?"

"Sure. You know how many millions of dollars in inefficiency this country loses every year because of drugs on military bases? More important, what kind of fighting capability do you think men on drugs have? It might stimulate them for a while, sure. The old Vikings sometimes used a psychedelic mushroom to make them feel like giants before going into battle. But it's not something that's useful for extended fighting or for military discipline. Those Vikings were almost as likely to hack each other up as their enemy. Men on heroin or strung out on speed—how cool are they in a fight or at doing the delicate mental work needed for electronic warfare? Drugs on military bases are widespread, a big problem. The guy who sold them to you is more than a pusher—he's a traitor to his country. Because the Army has to be ready at all times."

She shook her head. "You're full of surprises, Mr.

Sullivan. I took you for the strong silent type. But out comes this articulate lecture."

"If a problem pisses me off, I think about it. So should any man. Sure, I believe in machismo. But there's a machismo of the thinking man. Anyway, are you one of these people who thinks narcotics are just a harmless recreation, and it's okay if our armies are addicted and brain-fuzzed?"

She got up and left the table. He supposed she was offended. He shrugged and lit a cigarette. So let her sulk.

But there was the sound of a toilet flushing, and she came back. "That's that," she said, sighing.

"What's what?"

"I flushed my stash down the toilet."

He smiled at her. "Thanks."

"You mind if I call you Jack?"

"I don't mind." He got up and said, "I'll be right back."

He went out to the van. The crickets chirruped at him as he unloaded the weapons from the cache compartment. He carried the guns and crossbow inside. They were a heavy armful. He said, "Give me a hand."

She took the guns from him, whistling softly to herself, and laid them out on the kitchen table. He inspected them, and began loading clips. She helped him for a while, and her fingers showed a familiarity with all the weapons she handled. They discussed the virtues of the Skorpion as opposed to the Browning SMG, and he told her how to use the crossbow. As he helped her crank it to firing position, her hand brushed his, and a spark of sexual electricity passed between them.

He tried to ignore it. But it wasn't easy—he suddenly had a hard-on.

She had taken off her jacket, revealing a tight T-shirt over full, taut breasts, and a thick but curvaceous waist.

He cleared his throat and moved back to his chair, pretending great interest in the bore of an assault rifle. "How do these damn things get so dirty?" he growled. "I just cleaned them, and it hasn't been fired. Maybe there's an exhaust leak in the van . . ."

"Guess I better make some coffee—the approved 'speed'," she said just a little mockingly. "Want some?"

"Sure. Thanks."

As she made the coffee, she talked about herself. She was basically a country girl, one who'd belonged to the 4-H, who'd bred and raised horses, who loved nature and believed strongly in conservation. Sullivan, too, loved camping in an untainted wilderness, and they talked about that awhile. But there was a sense in the air that all this introductory talk was just a sort of polite attempt to do the proper thing. What she'd really have liked to do was—

Sullivan cut that line of thought. It was arrogant to suppose this girl was that much attracted to him.

But when she looked at him . . .

They sipped their coffee, and then she reached out and traced a finger along the scar on his cheeks. "This one looks like a bullet crease."

"Yeah," he confirmed, shrugging. "Not too pretty."

"I kind of like it."

That didn't surprise him.

She looked into her coffee cup and said, "Uh . . . how about if I show you your room? I mean, even if you're not going to sleep, you'll want to stretch out and rest."

"Okay," he said, against his better judgment. He finished his coffee, then followed her upstairs. He tried not to watch her ass move as she went ahead of him.

They went down a narrow wood-floored hall to the left and she opened a door, ushering him in. It was chilly, but a cozy-looking room, with a rug on the floor and antlers over the fireplace opposite the big old-fashioned four-poster bed.

To keep himself busy, he took some kindling from a wooden crate beside the gray-stone fireplace and built a fire, igniting it with his cigarette lighter. They watched it crackle for a while and then she turned to him and confirmed something he'd heard about the sexual aggressiveness of the Wacs. She ran a hand over his chest very suggestively. "Jesus, you're a big guy," she breathed. "You know, it's weird—I mean, maybe it's tacky to mention it, but just today I was looking at that *Soldier of Fortune* in the magazine store and ... uh ... I saw your picture and it started me thinking wouldn't it be nice if ... I mean, I had a sort of daydream ... And the very same day I meet you."

He gently pushed her away. "Look," he said. "You're attractive and I like you. But ... I try to take the advice of the Indian warriors. Before they go into a fight, they lay off sex. Celibacy makes them more keyed up and ... um, energetic. And since they were almost always going to go to war on one tribe or another, they were most always abstaining. Which made them good fighters."

"Sure," she said. "I knew it was too good to be true. Men never want a Wac. Threatens their masculinity."

She turned on her heel and he caught her arm, laughing.

"Hey, don't go away mad." He spun her around and kissed her, his lips parted, melting into hers. She was soft and giving when she moved against him. She did a little shimmy with her shoulders, rubbing her breasts against his chest.

Sullivan was only human.

"Okay," he said. "We have a few hours ..." He began to tug her T-shirt off her. She put her hands over her head to make it easy for him.

"But what about the Indians' advice?" she asked teasingly, running a palm roughly over the growing bulge at his crotch.

"This time I'll make an exception."

As their passion mounted, the undressing happened like leaves blowing from an autumn tree in a hurricane, and they were quickly on the bed, undulating together. She was a strong, athletic girl, and she surprised him by whispering, "Get rough with me ... a little bit.

Most men are so ... soft. I like it when ... when a man is stronger than me, takes control and ... *Oh.*"

He'd taken her two wrists in a single big hand and twisted to force her onto her belly, then grabbed her hips and jerked her back so she was up in kneeling position, ass toward him, perfect round white ass cheeks in complement to her breasts, which he cupped one at a time under his hands as he rammed into her from behind; breasts like extra-large grapefruits cut in half, but soft as whipped cream, the nipples hard in his palms. He pinched the nipples, sensing her need for a little pain, and she groaned, convulsively jacking back on his eight-inches, impaling herself on it again and again.

Later, after they'd rested, he took her from the front, using that special stroke which employed his belly muscles as a clitoral stimulant, till she came, flailing in his arms like a small trapped bird flapping to be free—but she didn't want to get free at all.

When he thought she was exhausted, and when he himself was feeling almost drained, when they were both slick with sweat and sticky with excitement, she turned on her belly and said, "Please—take me through the back door."

Excited by her submissive gesture, he felt his strength return to him, and his sword became sharp again. He lubricated her ass with her own juices, and plunged that sword home, using it as masterfully as any fencing expert.

There's more than one kind of warrior. Sullivan was both kinds.

Then they rested, and two hours later it was graying at the windows, near dawn.

The time for loving was done, for now.

Now it was time for killing.

The lovers would work together—to kill their enemy.

11

The Dawn Skirmish

"There are supposed to be two sentries," Milner
was saying. "One over there where he can watch the
approach from the woods and the fields as well as the
road . . ." He pointed through the washed-out dawn
light to the first bend in the road, just up ahead.
"He'll be just around that bend, unless they've changed
things. And one will be on the second floor, watching
the prisoners—maybe camped out in the hall. Then
there's supposed to be a guy just inside the kitchen
door watching the back. But the Swenson bunch are
lazy and disorganized. They just might be slacking off."

"Yeah," Sullivan said. "Like sleeping rattlesnakes."

They had parked the van behind a screen of brush
ten yards off the gravel road that led to the farmhouse.
It was a dead-end road, and there were no other houses
on it.

Sullivan, Beth, and Milner stood just off the road in
a stand of trees. Sullivan had the Heckler & Koch
assault rifle slung over his shoulder. On his hip: the
Colt .357. On the bandolier across his chest were two
hand grenades. Milner and Beth each carried an M16.
Milner also toted the Beretta and two grenades.

Birds chirped for the morning in the trees around them.

The ground mist was rising to its rendezvous with the sun, wreathing the tree trunks of the small deciduous woods on both sides of the road.

Sullivan tossed the smoking butt of a Lucky Strike onto the road and looked up at the top of a big, gnarled elm tree a few yards in front of him. "Dammit," he muttered, "it looks like I'm going to have to climb that fucker." After a night without sleep, he was in no mood to climb trees. He'd been climbing Beth's limbs for hours already. . . .

"What the hell," he said more briskly, "maybe it'll wake me up."

He took off the bandolier—it wouldn't be wise to get a hand grenade snagged on a branch—and laid the assault rifle aside. He grabbed the lowest branch that looked like it would hold his weight and, grunting, hauled himself up. After a few minutes of climbing, he "got into it." He remembered the feel of the tree limbs, resilient and alive under his hands when he was a boy. He'd climbed trees like this one to plant his own improvised flag atop them so he could see it from a distance, and think: I planted that flag there. That's my tree. That's my mark on the world.

He remembered the photo of himself as a young man he'd seen in Beth's copy of the *SOF,* and wondered again if there were anything left in him of that idealistic young man. That picture had been taken just before the young Jack Sullivan had gone off to Vietnam. And Vietnam had changed him forever. He'd found his vocation there—but sometimes he thought he'd left all his humanity there, too. And maybe that was part of the explanation for the moral fury that drove the older, warrior-wise Jack Sullivan to seek out evil and take vengeance on it for those it had brutalized. He was trying to regain his humanity.

When he reached the top of the tree, he felt almost exhilarated, refreshed, and ready for the fight. All the time knowing that this fight, like any other, could be his last. Not even the Specialist led a completely charmed life. It only took one bullet, even a little .22, or a fragment of one, to kill him if it hit him in the right spot. It could be a ricochet, a stray bullet from one of his buddies . . .

Or, for that matter, he realized, as he nearly lost his footing, he could fall and break his neck right now.

He clung to the trunk of the tree, using its main stem for partial cover, and peered over the treetops at the farmhouse. There was a thin stream of smoke, as from a dying fire, rising from the chimney. They were still there.

The house faced north. There was a meadow of high grass on the west side of the house. On the east side was a vacant lot piled with graying lumber and the skeletons of rusting car hulks. Good cover for approaches both east and west. He couldn't see the back clearly, but it looked like an extension of the grassy meadow, and then more trees. To the north of the house was a muddy front yard, bits of car junk scattered about it, a broken rabbit hutch to one side, and the gravel road. There was a black pickup truck, with its back roofed by canvas, parked out front. Sullivan frowned, surprised that Martindale hadn't gone to more trouble to hide the truck. Maybe this was the wrong place. Maybe he was about to burst in and blow away a bunch of innocent Okies.

But then, the truck could have been left in the open as part of the cover, as if to say: We've got nothing to hide. Which meant that Martindale had squared the occupancy with whoever owned the broken-down old house, renting under some pretext.

There was a narrow, rutted dirt road, just visible through the trees behind the house, probably leading to the fields that the house's former tenants had once tended.

Sullivan couldn't see the sentry. He watched for another five minutes, hoping to see him moving. Probably he was in under the trees that lay between Sulli-

van and the house, shielded by the tangle of gray
limbs and the sprays of new buds.

Sullivan climbed quickly down, formulating an attack plan.

He dropped from the tree and retrieved his weapons.
Milner and Beth were shuffling their feet restlessly
to one side. They were nervous. Milner was still
hobbled, and hadn't fought actively for a long, long
time. Beth had never seen real action.

Sullivan turned to them and said, "I can handle
this myself. You two are nervous, and that could blow
it. You could hold back and cover me if you see I'm
forced to retreat."

The pair burst out with a mingled stream of curses
and protests, both of them going red, until Sullivan
said, grinning, "Good—then come along. Maybe you're
less nervous now."

"But what are you going to . . . ?" Beth began. "I
mean, exactly how . . . uh . . . ?"

Sullivan said, "Well, I figure it like this. . . ."

Polonov was in that strange state of mind halfway
between waking and sleeping, where dreams sometimes overlap onto waking reality. He had been dream-
ing of the money. The five million dollars that he and
Martindale planned to split.

The night before that dream had commenced, they'd
learned from the newspaper-ad response that Bremmer
Inc. had agreed to pay the ransom. He'd gone to sleep,
only a few hours before, thinking of that money, and
that thinking had seeded his dreams.

He'd dreamed that he and Martindale had the heaps
of hundred-dollar bills, those understated-dull-green
U.S. dollars the whole world desired, lying on a table
before them. And he'd looked up to see Martindale
smiling that perfect smile of his, and in Martindale's
hand was a gun.

"Sorry, Polonov," he said. And just then, in the
dream, the door was flung open and Swenson came in,
laughing, machine gun in hand. . . .

The creaking of the boards woke Polonov completely. He sat up on the army cot and reached for his gun. The room was dark. A faint beam of gray-blue light cut through the window slats, showing whirling dust motes. Everything else was darkness—but there was a deeper darkness, in the shape of a man, at the doorway.

His .45 in his hand, Polonov rolled off the cot and came up in a crouch, six feet to one side, his gun answering the ack-ack and muzzle flash from the doorway. Tongues of flame licked at each other in the darkness. Polonov grunted, and for a moment he wasn't sure why. Then he felt the searing pain in his right side. The figure in the doorway had vanished— moved back to cover.

Wincing with the pain, Polonov got to his feet and moved to the farther corner, out of the line of fire from the doorway. He stood beside his pack—and bled on it. There were a flashlight and two extra clips of rounds in the pack. He took these, stuck them in his belt, leaned the pack against the wall, and stood on its aluminum rack as if it were a stepladder. There was an entrance to the attic overhead here, if he remembered correctly. Feeling like his insides were preparing to crawl out the burning hole in his side, he pulled himself up through the attic entrance. A thudding came from below as he drew his legs up into the trapdoor, and he felt a slug slash into the meat of his calf on his right leg. He gritted his teeth and pulled his legs up after him, forcing himself to ignore the pain. He brushed spiderwebs aside and drew the flashlight from his belt, fumbled at the switch and flicked it on, thinking: Swenson. Not Martindale. Martindale wouldn't have missed me. Swenson's men aren't good shots.

Polonov moved through the darkness of the attic, crawling over the rotting rafters, pulling himself along with elbows deep in the layers of insulating sawdust between the two-by-fours. And then, in the flashlight's yellow beam, he saw something impossible: the sawdust leaping up before him, dancing about, throwing itself in fountains at the roof.

Gunfire from below, hammering up through the ceiling. Hunting for him!

He rolled across the boards, which ran parallel with his body, swearing in Russian at the pain the bumpy movement brought. The firing stopped, as if his attackers realized from the sound of his movements that he was for the moment out of reach. He crawled along the places where the fittings under his hands told him he was over the walls between rooms. The flashlight beam fenced madly in his hand. His side was sticky and wet, his leg going wooden. There was sawdust in his mouth, and his throat felt like it was coated with sand. He kept going.

Martindale and Garcia were flattened to either side of the door of the room containing the radio, where Martindale had been sleeping. Martindale was wounded. The idiotic one, Gordon, had shot him in the left shoulder, and then missed again and again as Martindale had run for cover.

He wondered how Polonov was faring.

Then he heard them firing at the ceiling. Were they mad?

But it must be that Polonov had escaped into the attic. There was still hope, then. The three of them could surely wipe out this bunch of lunatics. After all, what did they need them for now? He had planned to wait, to use them for cannon fodder if the police came—let Swenson and his cronies take the police gunfire while he escaped out the back. But now Swenson's greed had certified that he must die.

All this the man who called himself Martindale thought, trying to keep up his nerve. But even as the blood flowed from his shattered shoulder, even as his arm grew deader, more numb, he knew the end was coming. He could feel its cold shadow falling over him.

"No!" he said aloud.

Garcia looked at him, startled.

And then a scraping movement in the hall alerted them. They raised their guns . . .

Someone ran past the door, firing.

9mm slugs struck the radio transmitter, shattering it like china. No chance of radioing for help.

Martindale gritted his teeth and nodded at Garcia. Both men cocked their Uzis and spun together to face the door, their weapons spitting fire and lead, rattling death for anyone in the way.

The rounds smashed in frustration into the wall, longing for flesh to cut and finding only plaster and wood. And then they caught a glimpse of Swenson at the head of the stairs to the left, grinning.

Martindale stepped into the hall, squeezing the trigger.

The Uzi was mute. He'd reached the end of his clip.

"It's the judgment of the gods!" Swenson shrieked, firing. At this distance, he couldn't miss. The submachine gun in Swenson's hands lashed a dozen 9mm tumblers through the Soviet agent's belly, cutting through him to splinter his spine and send him flying backward, screaming.

Garcia stood just inside the door, staring at the ripped-open body of his leader, the man he'd always believed immune to danger, to failure, to pain. The Soviet agent was squirming like an earthworm dying on a hot sidewalk, pawing listlessly at the place where multicolored entrails showed shiny and blue-red in the nine-inch wound.

And Garcia whimpered. The maniacs would get him. The maniacs . . .

There was an explosion then that shook the house and made dust spit from the doorframes. It sounded as if someone had blown up the front door. Swenson was supposed to be sentry—so there was none. And someone had found them . . .

Garcia thought: *The Specialist!*

And then he was no longer scared of the maniacs. They were nothing, in comparison.

Polonov hardly felt the explosion. He was feeling more and more removed. So weak, so weak . . .

It would be so easy, so beautiful, to relax, to lie here on the sawdust and go to sleep. . . .

No, you fool! You're dying! You've got to keep moving, get help! Get out! Go!

Riding the strength from a surge of adrenaline, he pulled himself forward again looking for another way out of the attic.

He hardly felt it when he dragged himself across a rusty nail end and it dug itself into the flesh of his leg, raking a long bloody gash. He kept on, making the gash longer, the flashlight nearly falling from nerveless fingers, the gun slippery in his other hand.

There! A square place . . .

A square place where the rafters ended. Another trapdoor, to another room.

He heard a noise behind him, a flash of light. There was a sound like a bee buzzing by him—a bullet! He looked over his shoulder, his heart pounding.

He saw an apparition: a beautiful woman; a head severed from its body. Only her head was there, staring at him, ghoulishly lit by streaming light from beneath. A dark-eyed woman.

Esmeralda. Climbing up through the trapdoor. Her hands came into view, an SMG in them.

He brought the gun around and fired. But he was shaky, and it was an awkward angle. The sawdust kicked up a foot to the right of her head. She ducked back down.

He pulled himself desperately ahead, and got to the trapdoor. He reached for it . . .

The trapdoor moved by itself.

No, someone was pushing it aside from beneath. He hurriedly backed off, feeling a brutal resurgence of the pain in his side and his leg, the two centers of hurt running together like a spreading fire.

There was a rattling sound from the trapdoor ahead of him as someone pushed it completely aside. He swung his flashlight around, and it spotlighted the grinning yellow face of Ortega.

Polonov raised his gun to fire . . .

Ortega was quicker.

Polonov felt the slugs rip into his neck and shatter the bones of his skull. All the strength drained out of him, and he fell gratefully into death. There was a second or two of sensory awareness before the end, and through the scarlet haze of pain he heard the woman shouting, "Someone blew up the front door, Ortega! Get over here!"

Polonov smiled, knowing who that must be. Then he died.

12

Catching Hell—and Letting It Get Away

Sullivan, on the roof, had waited till the front door had gone up in the plastic-explosives detonation. He had spotted a side window covered only with cardboard.

Now he lowered himself from the roof and found footing on the windowsill; holding on to the roof edge above the window with one hand, he kicked at the cardboard, knocking it away, and jumped through, the Colt in his hand.

A squat Hispanic guy with an Uzi was frantically slapping another clip into it, turning to face Sullivan. Sullivan snapped off two shots, one through the Hispanic's heart, the other through his forehead. The man stumbled back against the wall, slid to the floor, staring glassily into eternity.

Sullivan holstered the Colt and unslung the assault rifle, holding the automatic weapon at the hip like a submachine gun as he moved cautiously to the wall to peer into the hallway. He raised his eyebrows, seeing the gutted corpse of Martindale in the dim corridor. The narrow passage was murky with a blue-gray underwater light.

He heard a triple burst of gunfire from outside the house: that would be Beth, firing at the back door, keeping it secure. Hopefully Milner was covering the front, securing the enemy's escape vehicle.

Presumably the enemy's attention was chiefly directed to the part of the house where the explosives had ripped away the front door and the porch roof.

But presume nothing, Sullivan had learned, and you live longer.

Looking at Martindale's body, Sullivan thought: Very decent of Swenson to do part of my work for me. They must have gotten word from Bremmer Inc.—and Swenson decided to get rid of the KGB men before they got rid of him. It was the money, of course. Money had killed them.

Sullivan looked toward the room where Milner had said the hostages were kept. He thought he heard someone sobbing.

Then he heard a shouting: "Get up! Get fucking *up!*"

A man's voice, sounding tired: "I can't move very well—my legs went to sleep."

"You'll move or I'll blow the little cunt away!" A woman's voice. Probably Esmeralda.

Sullivan moved cautiously down the hall. He heard a rattle of SMG fire from below—one of the psychos firing through the blown front door at Milner, maybe. There was an answering fire, and then a back-and-forth dialogue of automatic firetalk.

Sullivan was four feet from the doorway he wanted when Swenson looked out. Swenson froze, seeing Sullivan; then he grinned. Sullivan's assault rifle leapt in his hand just as Swenson pulled back.

Sullivan cursed. Why had he waited that split second?

Swenson's eyes. The guy was hypnotic. His personality had made Sullivan waver for a moment. Sullivan gritted his teeth. That sure as hell wouldn't happen again.

There was a shadow in the doorway ahead.

Sullivan flattened against the wall to the right and raised the rifle.

This time . . .

His finger froze on the trigger as a young, frightened blond-haired girl showed in the doorway, pushed from behind. Then, behind her, came Esmeralda. The Bremmer girl was between Sullivan's gun and Esmeralda. And there was an Uzi muzzle pressed to June Bremmer's neck.

The lady psycho and her hostage stepped into the hall and began to move toward him. "Drop that gun, asshole," Esmeralda hissed.

Sullivan shook his head. "Let her go. I'm willing to shoot through her to get to you." That was a lie, but he hoped she believed it.

She didn't. She kept inching toward him. Behind her came Swenson, pushing Bremmer. Bremmer looked as frightened as his daughter, and his white hair was comically disheveled.

Sullivan's heart pounded as he struggled to make up his mind.

He could shoot past the girl and kill Esmeralda—he was sure he could do it without hitting June. But Esmeralda might pull the trigger spasmodically as she died. And there was Swenson to consider.

"We're going to kill them," Swenson said, "unless you drop that gun."

"No you won't," Sullivan said. "The place is surrounded, and you know it. You can hear the gunfire. You need them. You better be very fucking careful with those people, Swenson."

Sullivan backed up, into the door of the room he'd just left, stepping over Garcia's body at the same moment Esmeralda stepped over Martindale in the hall.

He kept the rifle leveled at the door as they passed. Neither side dared to fire.

Sullivan's plan, his timing, had been blown by the internal fighting of the kidnappers. He had counted on getting between the prisoners and the kidnappers and then trapping them between his fire and Milner's.

But it wasn't working. He had to improvise.

As the killers passed out of sight of the door onto the hall, Sullivan backed up and moved to the window. He slung the rifle over his shoulder and climbed out. He held on to the window frame with one hand and stood on the sill, teetering a little as he reached up to the roof with the other hand.

Back to high ground.

Milner was just inside the cab of the pickup truck, firing now and then through the open window, at the moment trying only to keep Gordon and Ortega pinned down inside the wreckage of the first-story house-front.

Flames licked around the ragged hole where the front door had been; they fed sluggishly on the wet, mildewy wood, but they were gaining ground. Soon there'd be a major conflagration. And then the sheriff would be out here.

He heard a repeated banging of automatic-rifle fire from the back of the house—sounded like Gordon and Ortega had tried to slip out back. Maybe Beth had gotten them. Anyway, they were distracted back there now. . . . This might be his chance.

He climbed down from the cab and ran, zigzagging, ignoring the blazing pain in his leg, to a smoldering stack of fallen lumber to one side of the door. He was preparing to move into the doorway when he saw the girl in the shadows. She came out into the light, blinking, her dust-streaked face marked by tear tracks, her eyes like a frightened animal's, her tousled hair blond—but patched with blood.

Milner saw Esmeralda, and then Bremmer, with Swenson behind him.

"You out there!" Swenson shrieked. "We're going to get in that truck! Anybody tries to stop us, the prisoners die!"

They shuffled across the porch, then stepped over

the fallen smoking boards, skirting the flames, moving slowly toward the truck.

They hadn't seen Milner lying on his belly by the heap of fallen lumber. He lay stone-still as they moved past him, and made up his mind.

He let go of his M16, left it lying on the ground, and poised himself to lunge as they passed him. They had their backs to him now. Milner focused on the two guns in the killers' hands.

He leapt up, lunged, and grabbed both gun barrels, feeling an electric thrill of success as his fingers closed over the muzzles. He wrenched them away so they pointed at the sky, screaming, "Run! I've got them! —*run!*" at the Bremmers.

Esmeralda shrieked and tried to twist the guns free. Swenson turned, snarling. The Bremmers, taking advantage of their captors' momentary surprise, twisted loose and ran, stumbling, helping one another up, to the corner of the house. Swenson ripped the gun from Milner's grip and turned it on him, bellowing, "Eat this eat this eat this!" as the slugs ripped into Milner's chest and he felt a giant fist punching him backward into a slow-motion spin. . . .

He had a spinning glimpse of Swenson and Esmeralda climbing into the cab of the truck. They were going without the hostages. The hostages were free. Were safe.

Milner died thinking: Maybe I made up for it, just a little.

Sullivan signaled Beth to move in, and then dropped from the corner of the back roof, falling fifteen feet to the wet ground. He heard the sound of running footsteps behind him and spun, whipping the Colt from its holster. He stared for a second, surprised, seeing Bremmer and his daughter running up, both of them weeping with relief.

"You . . . you're the police, aren't you?" Bremmer said brokenly.

"No," Sullivan said. "But I'm a friend—"

The crack of gunfire from behind made him whirl and press against the wall of the house. Gordon ran around the corner, panting, a gun in his right hand. His left arm hung limp, shot half away. Beth had caught him there.

Sullivan and Gordon looked at each other for a split second.

June Bremmer screamed.

Sullivan sent two .357 slugs into Gordon's brain and out the back of his head. Gordon fell back, the machine gun in his hand spitting angrily at the sky as his reflexes squeezed the trigger. Then he lay still and the gun was silent.

Sullivan heard a shouting from the front of the house. He ran that way, yelling at Bremmer, "Get down, flatten in the dirt!"

Sullivan ran between rusting car hulks and pulled up sharply at the front corner of the burning house. He peered around the edge just in time to see Ortega pile into the back of the truck as it fishtailed off down the gravel road.

Beth came out of the house through the flaming hoop of wood where the front door had been, firing, but the M16 was too big for her to shoot accurately as she ran, and its recoil threw her shots wide.

Sullivan's line of fire was blocked by a sagging corner of the fallen porch roof. He moved to a clearer firing angle—but it was too late. The pickup pulled around the bend. Gone.

"I'll get you," Sullivan said softly.

13

The Devil and His Angel Dust

They heard the wailing of the sheriff's siren long before the patrol-car was dangerously near.

"Let's get the hell out of here," Sullivan said to Beth.

She was staring white-faced at Milner's body. But she held up all right, Sullivan noted, pleased.

He turned to the Bremmers. "You're safe now. Just go up the road and sit down and wait. The cops will be here soon."

"Oh, God . . . oh, thank God . . ." June Bremmer sobbed, her face buried in her father's neck.

"I don't know how to thank you . . ." Bremmer began.

"Thank your mother," Sullivan said. "She hired me. But listen, when the sheriff gets here do me a favor, if you're grateful. Tell the cops that it was this guy"—he pointed at Milner—"who got you out. Your old friend Milner. That he wanted to even the score, because he felt wrong about the sabotage he pulled off. Say nothing about me: you never saw me."

"Sure, sure . . ." the old man said, shaken. He and his daughter began to walk up the road.

Sullivan and Beth trotted past them to the van and got in.

Sullivan started the van and backed it onto the road.

He was free and clear two minutes before the sheriff's car arrived at the gravel road.

"Swenson'll head for the highway," Sullivan said. "And that means through Lightning Corners."

But the Swenson Soldiers were compelled to make a detour for gasoline.

Johnny Jensen found out about it at nine o'clock. For Johnny, who usually stayed up all night, nine in the morning was almost bedtime. He was staring glassy-eyed out the window when the truck pulled onto the private drive. He didn't say anything about it to the four other men working behind him, making the angel dust at the long, scarred lab table on the second floor of the pink split-level house. He was too stoned to say anything and besides, he was mad at Brook and the other guys. The night before, when they started work, they'd said that they'd show him how to make the dust this time. But then Brook saw that he was stoned, that he'd been getting into the dust again, and told him, "Johnny, you dumb shit, I told you ten thousand fucking times: you make it, you don't take it. We make it to sell to people, that's all. You wanna get brain damage or what?"

Johnny, who'd just turned seventeen, said, "Gimme a break, huh? I only took a little, and it don't mess me up that much. I can see what I'm doing." And then he'd fallen over a wooden bench and smashed up a bunch of test tubes.

Okay, sure, the stuff distorted your sense of time and space. Made you misjudge things. Made you prone to wild impulses. Had caused a guy Johnny knew to put his head in a campfire.

But hey—did they have to get *paranoid* about the stuff?

So he'd stood at the window for hours, watching the sun come up, seeing the world change in the light, seeing its colors run like watercolors under too much water, and then the truck had pulled up.

Cops?

No, the people getting out of that truck didn't look like cops. Must be Buyers for the Goods, come to check it out.

Hey—great! He could go down there and check *them* out, and get to know them and maybe make friends and work for them and get rich and buy a big house and fill it with girls with big tits.

So he went downstairs.

"Fuck that Brook and that Lenny and that Jim and that old fart Calvin, who's probably a faggot anyway," he muttered, crossing the furniture-cluttered front room and opening the door onto the porch. "Fuck those . . ." He broke off, and froze.

These guys had big guns in their hands.

"Hello, young man," said the woman, smiling. They were all grinning. They were pleased to see he was scared.

And suddenly his mind did one of those flip-flops typical of the PCP-user. The angel dust turned him upside down, and he was no longer scared. He was impressed, and he was *into it*.

"Hey!" he said happily. "I bet you're gonna . . . You're gonna rip off the stuff, right? And waste Brook and them other pricks?"

Intrigued, Swenson and Esmeralda exchanged looks, then looked at the boy, raising their submachine guns meaningfully.

"Tell us about this 'stuff,' " Swenson said.

"The dust, man. Pounds of it. The money! They only got about four thou here, but—"

"Dust?" Ortega was moved to ask aloud. "Angel dust? I always liked that shit."

"Sure! Listen, I wanna help you, okay? I . . ." He broke off, staring at Swenson. Because Swenson was staring at him. Those eyes . . .

"You're Swenson!" Johnny burst out. "The cult killer guy!"

Esmeralda smiled; Ortega chuckled. Swenson glowed. He fed on recognition in any form.

"Hey!" Johnny said again, burning with admiration. A whole new day was dawning for him. "Hey, I always thought you guys were *cool*! Hey, you ever see *Texas Chainsaw Massacre*? That's my favorite movie! It was great when the guy used the chainsaw on that one big-titted bitch . . ."

He gave out an inarticulate yelp as Swenson knocked him down, on his way into the house.

"Wow!" Johnny bubbled, in admiration, "you guys aren't fucking *around*!"

Esmeralda laughed. "This kid slays me."

She stopped laughing when she saw the man at the head of the stairs with the shotgun.

The guy with the shotgun, Calvin, an aging hippie with a gray-streaked beard, made the mistake of talking instead of shooting. "What the hell you people doing, you got a warrant or—"

Ortega's SMG rattled briefly, and Calvin fell down the stairs, the shotgun bumping along ahead of him. Both came to rest in a puddle of blood on the floor. But Calvin was still alive.

"Wow!" Johnny Jensen exulted, even more impressed. He took a small vial of PCP from his shirt pocket, snorted some, and, through swimming senses, took great pleasure in watching Calvin, who'd always had snotty things to say about him, go through his death agonies. "Hey! Can I perform the cup-doo-grass?" he asked Swenson, pointing at the shotgun. "I mean, I'd like to ride with you guys—I can shoot, man! I ain't scareda nothing!"

Swenson laughed. He liked followers as much as recognition: one produced the other. "Pick up the gun, then."

Swenson stepped back to keep the kid covered, just in case.

Johnny picked up the bloody shotgun, wiped it on the groaning hippie's back, pointed it at the man's head, and pulled the trigger.

It was a real mess.

"Hey that's *great* . . . !" Johnny began. He broke off, hearing the shouts from upstairs. The men up there were arguing about what to do, and probably breaking out more weapons.

Swenson was a born managerial type. "Tell you what," he whispered to Johnny. "What you can do, kid—uh, what's your name?"

"John Jensen."

"Okay, Johnny, listen—you just take that gun upstairs, tell your friends you just shot the intruder, the one who shot your buddy here, and when they're faked out, you let 'em have it. That shotgun's got three more shells in it. We'll back you up. Right behind you."

"Wow! An initiation test, huh? All *right!*"

"Yeah. Go to it."

It worked like a charm. Johnny went up the stairs calling, "Hey, you guys, it's me, Johnny! I got Calvin's gun! Some guys with a machine gun got him, but I cut 'em down!"

Swenson and Ortega, clips replenished from the ammo sack Esmeralda carried, were about five steps below Johnny, pressed against the walls, grinning at one another. Swenson's tongue played teasingly between his teeth; he was a mischievous kid playing a prank. Now, this was fun. That cocksucker Martindale the Commie took all the fun out of things.

Johnny stepped onto the top landing and through the door to the right, to be greeted by disturbed male voices. "Hey, Johnny, what the fuck is going *on* down there?"

"That the cops or what?"

"No," Swenson heard the kid answer, "some guy trying to rip off the goods. Come on and check it out. I blew him away! I tol' you I'd be useful, man!"

"No shit? All right, we check it out—"

"Hey, Brook." Johnny's voice. Swenson chuckled, hearing the prelude to violence in the soft voice.

"Yeah, what?"

"Just this." And the shotgun thundered twice.

There were screams, and a third man with a thirty-odd-six rifle came running out onto the landing, trying to get the deer-shooter cocked.

Swenson said, "Hi!" to the startled red-haired stranger, and opened up his skull with the SMG at a two-yard range, so that red hair on bits of skull was pasted to the wall with even redder blood.

They went cautiously into the upstairs room.

Johnny was just finishing off one of the guys he'd shotgunned, bashing his head in with the butt of the weapon.

He looked up, grinning. "I did all right, huh?"

Swenson's sense of perversity urged him to shoot the kid down then and there, and if he had, Ortega and Esmeralda would have approved. But the kid's eyes were shining with admiration for Swenson, and Swenson liked that, so he said, "You sure did. You're one of us. I figure you always have been."

With four thousand bucks, with new clothes stolen from the house's closets, with an extra gun, and with a lot of PCP and a small stash of cocaine taken from the hippie's pockets, and the gasoline they'd originally stopped for, the Swenson bunch went roaring off down the road, high-spirited.

Okay, so they'd lost the five million bucks.

But they had dough, a truck, guns, drugs, and the promise of a lot of fun up ahead.

Swenson wasn't sweating about that big scar-faced guy who'd busted in on them. He was just some SWAT guy, or maybe a detective hired to get the Bremmers back. So okay, they *had* the Bremmers back. So the scar-faced guy wouldn't risk his ass chasing Swenson now. He was no problem.

14

Blazing New Trails of Terror

"We missed them somewhere," Sullivan said flatly.

They were on their way out of Lightning Corners, back along the road toward the farm they'd hit that morning. The van purred smoothly over the highway.

Beth, riding shotgun beside him, was frowning over a map unfolded on her knees. "Unless they go south on a lot of really small roads for miles," she said, "they'd have to come through Lightning Corners on this damn highway. I can't see 'em heading south, back toward New York. When the Bremmers tell their story to the cops, swarms of them are going to come up north looking for Swenson. There'll be more cops to the south than the north. They must know that. They'll probably head for Canada."

Sullivan shrugged. "Maybe they plan to hole up somewhere. Maybe they switched vehicles. Maybe they ditched the truck and set off across the country. They're crazy—they might do anything."

She sighed. "It's needle-in-a-haystack time, then. We might just lose them after all."

Sullivan shook his head. He could feel them near. His sense of destiny, of purpose, was thrumming powerfully in him. He knew he'd been brought into this for a purpose.

Beth looked up at him. "That one we both shot— was he the one who cut my cousin and . . . ?"

Sullivan shrugged. "I think so. But Milner said Ortega was probably in on it too." He glanced at her. "You've done your part. I can drop you off at your place. Take care of this thing myself. You helped a lot—"

"Forget it."

"You really helped, but maybe now it's better :

"Forget it."

Sullivan grinned. "Okay."

It was almost ten. They were both tired and hungry. Sullivan yearned for coffee.

But sleep? He couldn't sleep. He had let them get away, and that galled him. His nerves ached, his pulse raced, his heart pounded—all with the deep need to release the fury that was bottled up in him. It was Celia Bremmer's fury, and June Bremmer's fury, and Milner's and Beth's. Sullivan was its means of expression, and he was profoundly pissed-off himself.

It was a sunny April morning. Wheeling gulls, straying inland a little way to steal seed from the newly sown fields, caught the sunlight and danced in it. Except for the occasional ugly housing project or combination franchise restaurant and gas station, the countryside was prettily rural and fresh.

Both Sullivan and his quarry seemed out of place here. Some no-man's-land, Sullivan reflected, would have suited them better.

He was wrenched from these thoughts by the sight of a pickup truck with a covered-arch bed coming down the road at them. A man and a woman sat in front; Ortega would be in back. If that were the Swenson bunch.

The pickup came abreast and passed, its occupants casting hardly a glance at the black van.

"Did you see . . . ?" Beth began. Her question was answered when Sullivan whipped the van around in

an abrupt U-turn. Beth had to clutch at the dashboard
to keep her balance; the van's wheels complained
against the asphalt.

Then he was behind them, accelerating. They were
only thirty yards ahead. Sullivan could see Swenson's
face in the rearview mirror as the psycho checked out
the black van. He'd noticed the U-turn. The back of
the truck was dark. Sullivan thought he could make
out two figures in there, but he wasn't sure. It wouldn't
make sense. There should be only three of them left.
Did he have the wrong truck? Maybe that wasn't
Swenson's face he saw in the side mirror, after all. It
was far enough ahead he couldn't be absolutely sure.
He picked up speed, with one hand reaching down to
loosen the Colt in its hip holster. Beth had the M16 at
her feet under her leather jacket. She bent down for
it.

"Leave it there," Sullivan told her. "Cops ahead."

"Shit!" she said. "If the cops get 'em alive, they'll
just get away again."

Sullivan shook his head. In jail, in an asylum, or for
that matter sitting on top of the gold at Fort Knox,
Swenson was going to get it. Sullivan was going to
give it to him.

But the cops sure as hell were a complication.

There were two of them, with their highway-patrol
cruiser blocking the road in the right-hand lane. They
stood by the car with their hands on their guns, mo-
tioning for Swenson—if it were Swenson—to stop.

The truck pulled up, and the driver leaned out the
window.

Sullivan slowed behind the pickup, not coming too
near it. He wanted to be able to cut around to block
them if they tried to duck to one side of the cops. But
he was close enough he could see Swenson, definitely
Swenson, leaning out to talk to the cops in khaki.

Sullivan was surprised to see no sign of a gun in
Swenson's hand. Instead, he had binoculars.

Bird-watching binoculars.

To Sullivan's amazement, the skinny young thin-mustached cop waved Swenson on, indicating he drive around the cruiser. And smiled as he did it.

"Son of a *bitch*!" Sullivan burst out. He put the van into gear and angled to follow the pickup—but the two cops ran out in front of him, frowning, waving their arms.

Sullivan swore again. He couldn't run over a couple of well-meaning cops. There were deep ditches to both sides of the road—he couldn't go around them.

He had to stop. Which meant letting Swenson get away. But there was nothing else he could do.

One of the damn fool cops had his gun out, and had the sense to point it at the van's tires.

Sullivan pulled up, trying not to look as burningly furious as he felt.

"Yeah?" Sullivan demanded.

"Have to ask you to get out of the car and put your hands on—"

"Do you know who that was you let go by you just now?"

"We know that truck. Belongs to the North American Bird-Watchers Society. They had the identification and—"

"That was Swenson, dammit! Haven't you got the reports? Don't you know what he looks like?"

The cop frowned. "We were told to check all vehicles in connection with a shoot-up at . . ." He broke off, seeing the gun on Sullivan's hip.

He stepped back from the van and raised his gun, holding it carefully with both hands, chewing his lower lip between his teeth, which made it hard to understand him when he said, "Get out of the car *now*! Your hands behind your head. Don't go near that gun."

His partner went around to the other side. "Hey, you too, lady. Come on. Out."

Beth looked at Sullivan questioningly.

Sullivan sighed. "I've a registration for that gun. It's legal. Mind if I get the registration out of the glove compartment?"

The young cop chewed at a corner of his ragged brown mustache, then said, "Okay, let's have a look."

Sullivan opened the glove compartment, moving slowly so as not to startle these amateurs with their shaky trigger fingers, and fished out the registration. He passed it out to the cop on Beth's side, since he wasn't pointing his gun with both hands.

"It looks good," this rather pear-shaped, balding cop reported, holstering his own gun. "Says it's for a Colt .357. Because the guy does special bodyguard work."

The other cop's gun wavered but didn't lower. Finally he said, "So he's registered, so what? That doesn't mean he wasn't involved in all that shooting." He gestured with the gun barrel: *Get out*.

"You guys ought to get on the radio. Hear it?"

The radio was crackling for their attention from the car.

"That's probably the report to look for the very guy you let through here," Sullivan went on, getting slowly out of the van.

He stepped out onto the road. The cop backed up, then said, "Now, unbuckle that gunbelt. Let it fall."

"Sure."

Sullivan looked past the cop, down the road toward Lightning Corners.

Swenson was gone. Out of sight. Vanished.

Sullivan moved with syrup slowness to unbuckle the belt, but at the same time called across to Beth, who was just getting out of the van on the other side, "Hey, Beth, show Inspector Clouseau over there what you learned in the Wacs, okay?"

The cops looked at one another, puzzled.

Beth threw a startled wide-eyed look at Sullivan, and for a moment he was worried that she didn't have the nerve.

But she did. She shrugged and threw her weight onto her left foot, drove the boot on her right foot deep into the gut of the overweight cop on her side of the van.

The cop folded up, gasping, his face going stoplight red.

His partner did what Sullivan had counted on—he gaped at Beth and her victim. Just long enough. Sullivan stepped in, struck the cop's gun arm aside, and nailed him on the point of his chin with an uppercut.

The skinny cop was lifted off his feet, maybe halfway out of his boots, and fell over backward, gun flying into the ditch.

Sullivan whipped out the Colt and turned to help Beth—but she'd already snagged the other cop's gun and had him cold.

They cuffed the two cops together in the back of the cruiser. Sullivan drove it to a copse of trees on a tractor's dirt road between fenced fields. He concealed the cruiser in the windbreak and got out, his Colt in his hand. The fat cop locked his eyes on the gun and whimpered. "You got no need to kill us!" he whined. "We ain't no harm to you now! Oh, Jesus . . . oh, please . . . oh, no . . ."

He pissed his pants.

Disgusted, Sullivan turned away and shot out the radio. He holstered the pistol and got into the van, which Beth had brought up behind the cruiser.

And they drove off like the devil was nipping at their tailpipes.

But not all cops are incompetent. And when Swenson saw the unmarked cars beside the sheriff's cruiser on the far side of Lightning Corners, he knew that this time he'd never be able to bluff his way through. This bunch talking to the sheriff were definitely city detectives. That Bremmer scumbag and his bourgeois bitch daughter had probably given a full description to the pigs. And these pigs knew what they were doing. One look told you that.

So Swenson turned off at the side street before the cordon, whipped around a corner, and shouted. "Everybody out! We got to change vehicles fast!"

Jeff Bob Moreland was in the garage helping his

dad when he saw the strange guys with the guns running up. His dad was just closing the hood on the Chevy station wagon, after having replaced the spark plugs. "What the hell—?" was all his dad said before they shot him. He was hit in the shoulder and fell down on the oily concrete floor. Jeff Bob saw the red blossom on his dad's grease-stained T-shirt, and at first he couldn't believe it.

He was twelve, and it was hard for him to believe that strange people could drop in out of nowhere and punch holes through his father. Just like that. For no reason.

"Ortega, you dumb shit!" one of the men shouted. The short one with the wolfish eyes. "Did I tell you to shoot? If those cops heard that shot . . ." But no cops came. Maybe they thought it was a car backfiring, since it was only one shot. Maybe the semitruck noise on the highway had blocked off the sound.

They never came.

And the bald guy with the gun was standing over Jeff Bob's father. He was putting away the gun. He was taking out a knife.

Jeff Bob grabbed up a wrench and ran at the bald Mexican, shouting. He didn't know what he was shouting. He hit the bald guy on the elbow of the knife hand because he knew that would hurt a lot and make the knife hand useless.

The man dropped the knife, shouting with pain.

"Run, Jeff!" his father said weakly, trying to stand.

But the bald Mexican had knocked away the wrench and he was jerking Jeff Bob around by the collar, throwing him against the wall, and for a moment everything exploded. When he was able to see and feel again—it seemed like a long time, but it could only have been seconds later—someone was dragging him into his dad's car, shoving him in the back. And then he was sitting between the woman and a teenage guy, a long-haired guy with an "Iron Maiden" patch on his sleeveless denim jacket. That one looked a little familiar. Jeff Bob thought he'd seen him around town.

Just then Jeff Bob was feeling as if he were in a dream. He saw the garage wall receding as the car backed up, saw his dad lying on the floor, bleeding. He saw his dad move—and that brought Jeff Bob out of the dream. His dad was alive!

So Jeff could think about his own problem. He was a Boy Scout, and he'd been taught to stay cool and *think* in emergencies

He turned to the teenage greaser beside him. "Are you guys kidnappers? Am I kidnapped? Because my parents haven't got much money . . ."

The teenager in the denim jacket said, "Kidnappers!" and then made a kind of high-pitched hiccuping noise that was probably laughter. There was something weird emanating from this guy that made him scarier than all the others.

But the others started to become like him too, because now they were sniffing some white dusty-looking stuff into their noses, and it was changing them.

Drugs. Oh, shit, they're taking drugs. Jeff Bob had heard stories . . .

The short one was driving, having to stretch himself a little to see over the hood because Jeff Bob's dad was tall and had the seat adjusted way back. The bald one was in the front seat, rubbing his arm, every so often turning to glare at Jeff Bob.

"You shoulda let me kill him, he'll call in about the car, Swenson," the bald one said bitterly. So that was Swenson. He'd called the other one Ortega.

"You didn't kill him?" Swenson seemed startled.

"Shit no. I was gonna cut his throat when this kid bashed my arm and you started to shout 'Everybody in the car!' "

"You *jerk*! He'll call the . . . Fuck it, it's too late now," Swenson said. "You know what we're gonna have to do? And maybe it's not so bad. Maybe it's all lining up for us like a karmic unfolding."

"Yes," said the Gypsy-eyed lady. "Like a karmic unfolding."

"The world will pay for its sins against us," Swenson was saying. He slobbered a little as he talked, and his face, when he turned it to Ortega, was all twitchy like an excited dog. The drugs. There was a scary atmosphere in the car, something Jeff Bob could feel in the air, and it was getting scarier and scarier. They were getting crazy on the white stuff. "And this," said Swenson, "is how it will begin to pay: we'll take over this town. We'll get hostages. We'll demand money and safe passage out. We'll take the hostages with us so we don't have to run through the countryside ... we'll make the countryside run for us!"

They laughed, and Ortega switched on the radio. It blared a song from the rock band Obsession, "Johnny Paranoid":

There's a truth you can't avoid
Listen to Johnny Paranoid
Life will end in the burning void

Shakin' shakin' shakin' like a rock-'n'-roll chord

Better get your cut and cut for what you get
And if it didn't scream you didn't get it yet ...

Great, Jeff Bob thought. *Just what they need to hear.*

The wackos laughed, and turned it up.

The punk rock blasted through the car as the drugs took complete control of the killers. The drugs blew the common sense right out of their heads. They became wildly incompetent—and twice as dangerous.

They were driving on a narrow blacktop road between two cow pastures, the grass tipped with light green from the first rains of spring. Here and there small ponds showed steel-gray reflections of the ragged-edged clouds.

"Man, I'm fucking *hungry!*" Swenson burst out. "And there's our restuarant!" He pointed at a well-kept two-story farmhouse, newly repainted white with red trimming, a set piece with its border of trees and flowers amid the fields, a great red barn behind it.

Laughing at nothing at all, the killers turned in at the gravel road, the car swerving, fishtailing, almost going into the ditch as the stoned cult leader played with the steering wheel.

There was a man in the front yard pushing a gasoline lawn mower over the perfectly square lawn.

Jeff Bob was sad, seeing him. He looked like a nice guy.

The man wore a billed red cap and a red plaid shirt. He had a big nose and a wide smile. The smile was puzzled when he looked up to see the car coming down the drive, pulling up a few feet from him, the men piling out.

The smile went away when he saw their guns.

"Take him out," Swenson said. "The men got to be taken out. We keep women and kids for hostages 'cause they're easier to manage."

"Lemme do it!" said the teenager holding the shotgun.

The lawn mower chattered and growled like a dog with its back up as the man in the red cap backed away toward the house, trying to stall them. "Now, wait a minute, here, the sheriff's not too damn far away . . ."

"Go ahead, Johnny," said Swenson, like a father approving of his boy's naive eagerness. "Do it."

Johnny pointed the shotgun. "Lay down, mister." Johnny broke into giggles. "Lay down on the grass and shut your eyes and maybe I won't hurt you if you lie real still." Giggles again. "Maybe I'll just scare you. So lay still no matter what you hear, okay?"

Swallowing, the man did as he was told. He trembled, and his hands made into fists, then opened, then fisted again.

Then Johnny did what Jeff Bob was afraid he'd do. He did it with the lawn mower.

Jeff Bob covered his eyes, then put his hands over his ears to shut out the screams.

After that, Jeff Bob didn't look up for a long time, not till the car was moving again. He opened his eyes and saw there was a scared girl about his own age in the front seat, between Ortega and Swenson. "It's okay," Jeff Bob told her. "We're hostages. They won't hurt us." Looking out the back window, he could see they'd set the house on fire. It was burning like mad.

The teenage one was throwing up the food he'd just eaten, out a side window.

The woman, Esmeralda was saying, "It's all clear now. We must go to the town and find a great group of hostages. I've seen it."

"What about the scar-faced guy?" said Ortega. "I'm not so sure he—"

"He has gone far away and will trouble us no more," she said.

Which was proof that she had no psychic powers at all.

15

Lightning Hits Lightning Corners

Sullivan sat sipping coffee from a Styrofoam cup, his eyes on the highway.

They were parked in the lot of a Burger King at the edge of town; they'd eaten a lot of bad food, drunk a lot of bad coffee, and now Sullivan was having bad misgivings. He was worried about having brought Beth into this thing. She could get a stiff prison sentence for hitting that cop. And if someone found that cruiser, a description of their van would circulate to every cop in the county.

There just wasn't much time to set things right.

Then Beth saw the smoke. "What's that? This isn't the time of the year for field burning. That's a helluva big fire over there."

Sullivan saw it now too, between two identical ranch-style houses across the road. A column of gray-brown smoke undulated up into the April sky. He tossed the cup out his side window, started the van, and burned rubber.

Five minutes later they were idling a hundred yards from the burning farmhouse. A fire truck had already pulled up and was pumping an arc of silvery water

131

into the upper story of the burning house. The flame would stick its fluttering red head out the window, as if mocking defiantly; the water would slap it back inside, steam and smoke would gush, and then the flame head would mockingly reappear.

"Completely out of control," Sullivan observed. "But maybe Swenson's bunch hasn't been gone long. There's a gas can on the lawn there, and gasoline would start it up quick."

"Maybe it wasn't them," Beth suggested. "Maybe it's a coincidence."

"There's a body on the lawn, covered with a blanket. See it! There's so much blood soaking through—that's not a fire burn. It must've been them."

The sheriff hadn't arrived yet. He was probably still counting the bullet holes at the deserted farmhouse where Sullivan and Swenson had done their respective work that morning.

Sullivan climbed into the back, opened up his hidden cache, and took a black box out of it. In the box was a sheaf of forged identity papers and fake passports—his emergency getaway system. There was also an FBI badge in the name of Richard Stark. That had cost him dearly. It was clipped into a wallet, with other papers for the mythical "Richard Stark, Special Agent."

He put on a suit jacket and dark glasses and hoped he looked the part. The badge probably wouldn't have worked on the highway-patrol cops; they're trained to detect fakes.

He climbed out of the van and strolled over to the iron-haired man who looked like he was in charge. He wore a yellow water-slick coat; there was a fire captain's badge on his chest.

"Say, Captain," Sullivan said. He showed the FBI identification. It passed. The man looked up with respect and curiosity. "You think this was arson?" Sullivan asked.

"Sure as hell was. The wife saw them set the thing

on fire. She's in hysterics. We sent her to a hospital already. They didn't see her. Killed her husband, though. Ran him over a few times with a power mower."

Both men winced.

Sullivan said, "Three or four of them, were there? A short guy, a bald guy, a woman . . . ?"

"That's right. You looking for them?"

"That's why I'm here," said Sullivan truthfully. "They were in a pickup, right?"

"No, a Chevrolet station wagon. Green and blue. Big one. The short guy driving. They took the daughter of these people here as a hostage. They had a little kid with them already, a boy. Probably another hostage."

Sullivan frowned. "Which direction they take?"

"Back toward Lightning Corners. Toward town center. We already called in . . ."

But Sullivan had turned to run back to the van.

Jeff Bob was trying not to be scared. The lawn-mower thing, though. It was hard not to think about that. That was the sort of thing you saw in your worst nightmares.

And the girl—her name was Marleen, he'd learned that much before she'd lapsed into hysteria—she kept sobbing and sobbing.

Until Esmeralda started hitting her. "Shut up, you sniveling cunt! Your dad was a pig and you should be glad he's dead!"

The others in the car howled with laughter at this. The girl covered her eyes and bit her lip to keep the sobs inside.

Johnny and Swenson were singing atonally along with a golden-oldies song on the radio. "I can't get no sat-is-fact-chun . . . Oh, I try, and I try, and I try try try!"

They were careening up the main street. Cars were swerving to stay out of their way, crashing into trashcans and lampposts and one another as Swenson drove up the oncoming-cars lane against the traffic, shouting, "We're gonna get us some satisfaction today!" He tooted up a little more cocaine mixed with angel dust. The coke made him beam with megalomania. The angel dust seemed to make him swell up like a balloon filling with water.

Esmeralda had pulled out a few hanks of the girl's hair and bitten a piece out of her ear. The girl shrieked and clutched at her torn ear. Esmeralda lost interest in tormenting her. The greasy teenager, Johnny, was swigging from a bottle they'd taken from the house they'd set on fire. Southern Comfort.

Jeff Bob took a deep breath. To keep from losing his courage, he took charge of Marleen. He leaned forward and whispered to her, "You said your name was Marleen, right?"

She nodded, her eyes big, her head twisted around to see him over the back of the seat.

"Look, Marleen, we got to be smarter than these people or they're going to hurt us. We got to be real cool, because they're real crazy, right? And then we'll see a chance."

Marleen's eyes filled again. "My dad—"

"I know. But if we don't keep cool, we won't get the chance to make sure these creeps get theirs for hurting your dad. Right?" He smiled.

She nodded.

And then Swenson said, "I got a bi-ig idee-uhhhh!"

He jerked the wheel around and drove across the sidewalk.

"What you doing, Swenson, you crazy fucker!" Ortega burst out, covering his eyes as the car rammed through the big plate-glass window of a hardware store.

Glass exploded around them; things crunched and clattered and everyone jerked with the sudden stop of the car as it plowed into a shelf of hardware goods and then hit a wall.

There was a tangle of people inside the car for a while, along with steam from a cracked radiator, screams of terror from Marleen, and whoops of laughter from Johnny. But no one was really hurt. Swenson had a cut over one eye where he'd banged into the steering wheel, but he didn't seem to feel it much. He joined the laughter, all four of the nuts laughing, and then said, "Come onnnn!" He forced the door open and climbed out. A sputtering round-faced man in overalls was staring at the wreckage of his store. He turned to Swenson to demand "What the hell—?" and Swenson reached into the car, pulled out the submachine gun, and split the guy open from stem to stern.

Marleen shrieked and covered her ears against the sound of the gunfire. Her terror was infecting Jeff Bob. He whispered urgently to her, "Come on, get a hold on yourself, Marleen, remember what I said!" and he shook her shoulder. After a moment she quieted and nodded to him, her lips pressed to white.

"Get out the car, kid," said Johnny.

Jeff Bob nodded back at Marleen, and they climbed out, standing in the rubble under Esmeralda's guard as the others rummaged in the hardware store.

A police siren yowled up the street.

"Esmeralda!" Swenson called. "Show 'em the hostages!"

Jeff Bob and Marleen were displayed at the broken window, to one side of the jutting rear of the station wagon. Esmeralda stood over them, submachine gun in hand. Johnny leaned against the wall to one side, cradling the shotgun in his arms, drinking Southern Comfort.

The cops pulled up in their patrol car across the street. They got out—and froze in their tracks when they saw Esmeralda press the gun to the little girl's head.

"One move and they're splashed all over, like a busted jar of strawberry jam!" Johnny said, thinking himself very imaginative.

"We are the servants of Siva!" Esmeralda shouted.

Jeff Bob and Marleen did their best not to move.

Swenson came out of the rubble of the store carrying something in his arms. "Get back in your car, cops!" he shouted at the highway patrolmen.

They looked at one another, then at the children, and they got back into the car.

Swenson spoke in a soft aside to Johnny and Esmeralda. "When I throw the stuff, you grab the hostages and get down."

Esmeralda nodded. Johnny looked at him slack-mouthed, too stoned and drunk to comprehend quickly.

Swenson shouted, "Cops! Do a U-turn and come around here and we'll parley!"

The cops held a quick conference, then nodded affirmation at Swenson, started their car, and swung it around so it was snugged up against the curb, parallel-parked a few feet from the wreckage of the window.

In the ten seconds this had taken, Swenson had lighted the fuses on four sticks of dynamite bound together with twine.

Jeff Bob grabbed Marleen and pulled her down behind a crust of concrete wall where the station wagon had plowed through the frame of the window. He looked up just long enough to see Swenson pitch the dynamite through a side window of the cop cars. He ducked his head as Esmeralda, Swenson, and even Johnny took cover. The cops scrambled to get out of their car.

They didn't make it.

The car lifted up from the ground as if hopping, its windows vomiting flame and smoke, its roof flying off. The cops simply disintegrated.

A ball of flame consumed the car, and Swenson stood laughing as it rained bits and pieces of everything that had been in it.

"It's raining cops!" Johnny howled, laughing.

He snorted up some more dust.

Jeff Bob grabbed Marleen's arm and tried to make a run for it.

But Esmeralda's long, thin, whip-strong arm snapped out and wrapped around them both and threw them sprawling on a heap of broken glass. Jeff Bob's hands were cut badly; Marleen's right cheek was lacerated. They got up from the glass heap, and he pulled glass splinters from her face as she wept.

"Now," Swenson said, "the *real* fun begins."

16

Death Comes to the Town Meeting

"They keep trying to help," Sullivan observed, "and they keep getting in the way."

There were more cops up ahead.

He sighed. "What I wouldn't give for a good chopper. Can't fake 'em out with that FBI badge. It's not a very good counterfeit. They might call in to check the number. And word might've gotten around about this van if those plowboys we put on ice have been found."

"So that means . . . ?"

"We got to go through 'em or around 'em." He looked at her. "Seriously, Beth, this is the time for you to take a hike."

"We've been through this, Sullivan."

He pulled over at a gas station, by the bathrooms, as if he were there for that alone. They were blocked from the sight of the cops here.

He turned on the radio and was about to switch to the police band when he heard a report on AM radio news: ". . . four gunmen, including a woman, have taken over a Town Hall meeting in the small town of Lightning Corners. The meeting of eighty-five people was in progress when the gunmen burst in and—" A wave of static canceled part of the newscast. He heard only the tail end: ". . . reportedly demanding one million dollars in gold and free passage to a country of their choice in exchange for the hostages. The hostages include a boy and a girl—" More crackle. Sullivan turned it off.

He sat back thoughtfully and lit a Lucky Strike.

"Oh, Jesus," Beth breathed. "I think my uncle and aunt are at that meeting . . ."

Sullivan reached out and took her hand. "We'll get 'em out. All of them."

"But we . . ." She shook her head, and stifled a sob.

"Come on . . ." He looked at her, grinning. "Is this the tough woman who put a bullet in one of the most dangerous killers in the country and then calmly disarmed a highway patrolman? Huh?"

"I guess it isn't," she said, squeezing her eyes shut. "I guess it's some other girl."

"It sure as hell ain't a sergeant in the Women's Army Corps," he growled.

She stiffened, then wiped her eyes, took a deep breath, and said, "Okay. Let's do it."

"Good." He squeezed her hand. "But not yet. They're real tense now, waiting for the answer from the cops. It'll take a while. Hours. Some negotiator will try to talk them out of it. Then maybe the government will go through the motions of getting them what they want. Meanwhile they'll fly in a SWAT team. The SWAT team might do the job—or they might blow away a bunch of innocent bystanders. I think I'm better qualified. We're going to wait awhile, maybe an hour, till Swenson starts to get bored and careless. Then we find a way to penetrate the town. . . . You know this Town Hall?"

She nodded. "I could draw you a pretty accurate plan."

"Good. Get to it."

As she sketched out the plan, a service-station attendant came to the van's driver-side door. Trying to be gruff, he said, "Say . . . uh, you can't just park your van here all this time . . ."

Sullivan fished in a pocket and came up with a fifty-dollar bill. He passed it through the window. "You can keep that if we're not disturbed in any way for the next four hours or so."

"Huh? Oh, sure I . . . Oh, sure!" He took the money and left. Sullivan rolled up the window and pulled the curtains.

They pored over the Town Hall layout for a while, and Sullivan mentally roughed out a plan, then an alternate plan, and then contingencies.

After a time he looked up, surprised by the expression on Beth's face.

"Some people," she said, "can't think about sex when they're upset. But for me it's always been a release. A way to escape for a while. And we've got an hour. Now, I know what the Indians advise, but . . ."

"The hell with the Indians," he said, taking her shoulders in his big hands and drawing her near for a rough kiss.

They moved into the back. It was a little constricted for undressing, but they laughed off the awkwardness and stripped.

She was something molten in his arms, flowing against him, rubbing her full breasts up and down the length of his body, taking them in her two hands and using them to stroke his gunmetal-hard cock, running the tip of her tongue, then the tips of her nipples against the head of the shaft till he—the unbreakable warrior—groaned and moved back to escape her.

She giggled and came at him, straddling him, she on top, he on the bottom; she stroked the sticky-wet lips of her labia suckingly on his member as he pulled her down to suck her tongue between his lips.

"Fuck yourself with it," he commanded her, pinching her nipples cruelly . . .

An hour later she was refreshed and ready to face the fight.

They lingered ten minutes more for afterplay, then

Sullivan gave her a final kiss and tossed her clothes over. They dressed, and he opened up the weapons cache. They'd be setting out cross-country.

And this time he'd use the crossbow.

Jeff Bob felt better here in the Town Hall, with all the other people there. Normal people. He was still a captive, and still directly under Esmeralda's gun, sitting at her feet on the stage edge—but there were other captives here, and grown-ups.

He hadn't kidded himself into believing what he told Marleen: "It'll be okay now—they're making a deal with the cops and they'll have to let us go soon as part of the deal, see?" He knew that Swenson would take him and Marleen as hostages till they were safely out of the country. They were smaller and weaker than adults, and people were more careful about not hurting children. And he knew that sooner or later Swenson would probably kill him. And Marleen.

He'd known a guy like Swenson. A kid down the block. The kid had set cats on fire because he liked to watch them run and scream. Swenson, though grown-up, was that kind of kid.

So if Marleen and he were to get away, it would be because they did it themselves somehow. He kept telling himself that the chance would come.

Town Hall was a big, squarish place, a former church, with peeling white-painted walls and a podium at one end, on the short stage where the altar used to be.

Folding gray metal chairs had replaced the pews. The eight-five hostages sat in the chairs, slumped or rigid, grim-faced or weeping, angry or frightened. All of them let their eyes stray occasionally to the submachine guns in the hands of the man and woman on the podium, the shotgun in the hands of the grinning, idiotic boy at the side door, the killing machine in the hands of the bald Hispanic guy at the front.

The two kids sat beside the podium at Esmeralda's feet as she babbled quasi-visionary drug-induced pronouncements.

"You are the witnesses to the beginning of the apocalypse, wherein the Lord Swenson pays the world back for its evil repression and balances the Karma account! He is the instrument of God! He is . . ."

Swenson, the "instrument of God," was drooling and staring glassy-eyed out over her captive congregation, one arm cradling his submachine gun, the other in his pants as he masturbated absently.

"I got an idea from on high!" he bellowed suddenly, making the old women squeal and all heads swivel toward him. "I have seen it!" He took his hand from his pants and reached for the crate of dynamite he'd taken from the hardware store—normally used by farmers for blasting stumps and boulders.

Carrying the closed crate by the rope handle on one end, he walked toward the door behind the stage. "I'm going up to the roof to have a talk with the angels!" he shouted over his shoulder.

Johnny Jensen made a sound like *Hyuk Hyuk Hyuk*—and then cut the laughter off when Esmeralda glared at him, making him realize that Swenson wasn't kidding.

Swenson took the stairs that led up to the little wooden bell tower in the roof. On the way he stopped long enough to snort cocaine and PCP. Then he started climbing again, grinning, and carrying the dynamite.

There was an empty lot behind the service station, destined to become another housing project. Sullivan and Beth trudged across it, concealed from the cops at the cordon by the service station and a House of Pancakes. It was well that they were concealed, because they were carrying what were clearly automatic weapons, as well as a crossbow.

The ground had been stripped of turf and flattened in preparation for laying down foundations. Sullivan's boots sank into the rain-softened earth. He was glad when they reached the end of the patch of stripped earth and could climb over a short wooden fence onto a dead-end side street. They were a half-mile from Town Hall.

Clouds were thickening, and the wind had picked up. There was an electrical tension in the air that hinted an impending storm would soon blow in off the sea.

They slipped into a narrow gravel alley between rows of one-story bungalows. Dogs barked at them and small children gaped through the slats in back fences. When they came to a street they looked up and down, waiting till there were no cars in sight, then sprinted across it, gear clacking. If a cop or a "civic-minded citizen" saw them, they might be taken for members of the New Mind Liberation Army. They just might be shot down.

At last they were in sight of the white block of the town meeting hall. It was a cracker-box building, though two-story; at one end of the roof was a twenty-foot square-cornered steeple containing a rusted, disused bell and a crust of green-blue pigeon droppings—and Swenson.

There was a chain of heat around the old wooden building; cops and cop cars of every description: NYHP, Sheriff, NYPD, Lightning Corners Security Patrol. There was also a crowd of onlookers which every so often the cops would try to disperse.

Sullivan wondered how long it would take for the helicopters to come.

The SWAT teams were already piling out of a blue-white police transport truck, wearing their protective vests, helmets, carrying rifles and communications equipment.

Swenson was about a block and a half away from Sullivan's position, and three stories up, a melodramtic figure in the bell tower, like some mad Captain Ahab capering in the yardarms, waving his arms and shouting, laughing, exulting.

"How are we going to get through all these peple?" Beth asked. "And if we *do* get away with it—how do we get away with it? I mean—"

"I know what you mean. We'd be acting as vigilantes, illegally, under the noses of all those cops. We'd be arrested. I know. I'm committed to that. But you—"

"Are you going to start that again?"

He turned to her, his face hardened. "I thought you were ready to take orders. Have you lost all your military discipline? Sometimes the best strategy for a certain part of the fighting force is to stand down and wait in the background until they're needed."

"No. I'm sorry: I'm commiting mutiny, but I don't care. I . . ." She paused, swallowed hard, looked away. "I've been waiting for you for years, in a way. If you're going to be killed, so am I. If you're going to be arrested, so am I. I love you!"

Sullivan's heart sank. And that was the paradox of a man in his position. When a beautiful, desirable, loyal girl like this one tells a man she loves him, the man should be happy. He should feel great—not this sinking feeling.

But Sullivan knew that people who stuck near him sooner or later caught some of the gunfire meant for him. A woman who loved him would want to be near him. And that would be death for her. Plain and simple. It had happened before. . . .

"Shit," he said.

"Oh, thanks. That's the reaction I get when I tell you I love you. 'Shit.' Well, that's just great. I mean, I didn't expect you to pick me up in your arms and declare eternal love, but . . . 'Shit'?"

He smiled. "Sorry. I didn't mean it like it sounded. I could fall for you, Beth. It's a cliché but it's true that a guy like me can't get close to people. It's a risk for them. It's more than a risk."

"I don't care. I'm going in with you."

He nodded resignedly, "Okay. Let me think."

They were standing beside a tavern, half-hidden behind a dumpster overflowing with empty bottles and napkins. To their left the narrow alley was flanked by a kindergarten building, long and low and fashioned in that low-expense "modern" design that uses lots of picture windows and pastel panels; the windows were crowded with crayon drawings of spring flowers. The children had been evacuated. "Come on," Sullivan said. He led the way across the blue-gravel alley to a low hurricane fence around the kindergarten play area, opened the gate, and went in, Beth close behind.

They stashed the long-range weapons inside a playground crawl tunnel.

"We're going to have to take a chance those cops we iced aren't loose yet," Sullivan said. His Colt was fitted into a rib-cage holster inside his coat; Beth carried the Baretta tucked in her motorcycle jacket. "Let's see how close we can get for a reconnoiter."

They left the playground area and strolled casually out of the alley and across the street to join the crowd of gawkers. They heard Swenson's shouting, clearer and clearer as they approached.

"I'm not fucking around, you sons of bitches!" he bellowed. "I know you're setting up snipers to pick me off up here right now. Go ahead! If I get it, my friends have orders to blow away those two bourgeois puppies down there!"

Sullivan noted two plainclothes cops in dark glasses look at one another in consternation at this last warning. One of them ran to the car and barked orders into a radio, probably restraining his snipers.

"I'm warning you: get those fucking police cars out of here!" Swenson shrieked hoarsely, his voice coming in a thin echoing whine from on high, like a petulant sky god. "I want those SWAT teams out of here!"

"He's done a smart thing, the cunning little prick," Sullivan muttered. "If he stayed with the others it would be easier for them to break in and use quick-hit SWAT tactics to knock out him and his people before they had a chance to waste the hostages. But this way he's got a control. He can see them coming from up there, so if anyone approaches he'll warn his crew and the hostages will get it."

"I warned you about those pigmobiles!" Swenson

shouted. He pitched something from the steeple, which fell end over end to fall just short of a police car. A stick of dynamite.

The blast was felt in the air as a shock wave, and then it was heard—ka-*pock!*—and the crowd screamed, running helter-skelter. Sullivan and Beth had to take cover behind a police car to avoid being trampled.

There was another explosion, and another, as the giggling madman tossed sticks of dynamite down at the world. That's who he was really attacking—the whole world.

The cops swore, and flattened themselves on the ground, well away from the cars. No one dared to return fire, for fear of causing the death of the hostages in the meeting hall. They could be shot at and blown up—and couldn't do anything about it.

"Reminds me of a certain situation in Beirut a while back," Beth remarked, ducking her head as another stick of dynamite exploded.

Bits of turf from the park grounds around the hall were picked up in the blasts and tossed in the air, raining on the cars and helmets of the cops below the bell tower.

Swenson made an extra effort, and two bound sticks of dynamite fell neatly onto the windshield of a cruiser.

"Get back!" someone screamed.

The car jounced on its shocks as a fireball engulfed its front end, the window spattering every which way, pieces of glass propelled to slice into the exposed face of a nearby rookie, who screamed, blinded forever.

Swenson's laughter echoed through the ringing of the explosions.

He kept lobbing dynamite, soaring a direct hit on three more cars, turning them to useless hunks of flame-licked scrap metal. One by one the cars exploded again as the flames reached the gas tanks, arching their metal beds and breaking open from inside, spitting their metallic guts out to rupture flesh and break windows a block away, exhaling great folds of flame-streaked black smoke which blew acridly across the ravaged park.

The little town green was beginning to look like no-man's-land.

The SWAT men had moved back as their truck exploded, with most of their equipment in it. They stood in a frustrated cluster behind a barricade, arguing with their captain, demanding to be allowed to get the bastard.

"Okay," Sullivan said, "I'm going to try to—"

"No you're not," said a deep voice behind him.

He spun, reaching for his Colt. But the man behind him had a gun ready.

Sullivan froze, not willing to risk Beth—and reluctant to fight a cop.

And then he recognized the guy.

"Holstead!" Sullivan blurted.

The black man holding the .45 on him grinned. He was a stocky man with deep wrinkles around his eyes, and a big round face, his kinky hair clipped as short as it would go without the barber nicking his skull. He was wearing a suit with no tie, and in the hand that wasn't holding the gun was an FBI badge.

"Well, hello, Sullivan. I saw you sneak up here and figured you for some kind of vigilante—didn't see you clear till now."

"So now you know who I am, you can put away the gun," Sullivan said.

"Uh-uh." Holstead glanced at the bell tower. Swenson, seeing the cops retreat, had stopped tossing TNT. He was leaning against the bell, panting, a submachine gun in his hands.

Holstead looked back at Sullivan. "I'm supposed to run you in if I see you. Connection with some busted-up cruisers in Manhattan. Some guy squashed in a garbage truck. Little things like that."

"Can't let you do it, Fred," Sullivan said softly. "Much as I'd like to help you beef up your probably empty arrest record. But I'm gonna get that asshole"— he nodded toward the belltower—"no matter what."

Holstead nodded slowly. But he didn't put the gun away. He looked at Beth. "Who's this?"

Three other cops had walked up, one of them in uniform, drawing their guns. "What the hell, Holstead, who's this and what the fuck are you doing with him? You gonna talk at him or arrest him?"

"Well, I haven't made up my mind about that," said Holstead. The other cops looked annoyed, but held back. So it seemed Holstead was in charge. "I asked you a question, Sullivan. Who's the girl?"

Sullivan shrugged. "I don't know. Some local girl."

Beth looked irritated but said nothing.

"Bullshit," Holstead said. "She's packing heat, and any jerk can see she knows you for more than 'good afternoon, stranger.' I'd say she has the bad judgment to be in love with you."

Beth glared. Sullivan winced. Holstead laughed.

He and Sullivan were old friends, and the gibes, even in this tense situation, were friendly. Holstead had been a captain in Nam, and had more than once sent Sullivan on the missions that earned him the nickname the Specialist.

"Okay," Sullivan said. "She's a friend of mine. She hasn't done anything."

"Not even kick a trooper in the belly and handcuff him to his own car?" Holstead asked, grinning.

"Oh. No, that was me—" Sullivan began.

'Dressed as a woman? Sullivan, you'd be a lousy female impersonator."

Beth had to smile, despite the fact it was obvious to her she would probably go to jail soon.

Sullivan said, "Listen, Fred, those turkeys let Swenson through their cordon! They had him and they let him through because they thought he was a fucking *bird*-watcher!"

Holstead nodded. "I know. That's why I'm going to pretend I never saw this lovely lady. You *do* have good taste, Sullivan. So—"

"Now, wait a minute," said a state trooper standing

nearby, gawking back and forth between the two men. "If this woman attacked one of my men—"

"Harvey!" Holstead said suddenly, barking at the trooper. "Remember that time I got you out of that little trouble out on Long Island?"

The trooper swallowed, and stared at him. "Well, what's that—?"

"What it's got to do with it is this: you owe me a favor. So forget about the kick and the handcuffs and the whole bit. Tell your turnip-heads the girl got away. They sure as hell *did* fuck up, and we got some dead men and a lot of blown-up cars here to prove it!"

Harvey shut up.

Sullivan and Beth exchanged looks of relief. "Okay," Sullivan said, turning to Holstead. "You going to lower that gun?"

"There's still the matter of that skylarking you pulled off in Manhattan."

"The guy in the garbage truck was a Soviet agent working with that scum," Sullivan said, jabbing a finger at Swenson.

Holstead raised his eyebrows. "That's pretty wild stuff, Sullivan."

"If his prints are left—or his partner's face—you ought to be able to identify them. Run a check, and you'll find out they're working for the KGB."

"Maybe. But we don't know every agent in the country. And anyway, that would take too much time," Holstead said, shrugging. "So I guess I'm going to have to trust you right now."

He holstered his gun and laughed, clasping Sullivan in a bear hug.

Sullivan grinned and returned the hug. Army buddies never forget.

"Now, wait a minute, Holstead," said one of the FBI men. "You can't just—"

Holstead interrupted. "Gentlemen," he said, turning to the cops and feds clustered around them, "I have the honor to introduce to you . . . The Specialist."

Sullivan rolled his eyes at heaven. "A goddamn

plastic-surgery job," he muttered to himself. "Painful and expensive."

But Beth beamed with pride when she saw the looks on the faces of the men staring at Sullivan.

One of the men cleared his throat, and Sullivan knew he was going to ask for an autograph. That would be just too damn much.

Sullivan pulled Holstead aside. "Holstead . . . Fred, buddy . . . you know I can do it, if you give me the chance. I need one backup man who'll take my orders. A good shot."

"What!" Holstead said, as if outraged. "You expect *me* to let an unauthorized person, in defiance of all laws, take on a *police mission*?"

Sullivan grinned. "Precisely."

Holstead shrugged. "Okay."

17

Two Kinds of Madness, Two Kinds of Killing

Jeff Bob was staring at the string.

The string ran from the podium, where Esmeralda slumped wearily, across the stage, through the door behind the stage, and up the stairs to the bell tower. There was a small cow bell—used to call order for the town meetings—attached to the string, which was nailed to the side of the podium. Ortega had set it up at Swenson's command. The string at the bell-tower end was attached to Swenson's wrist. If he failed to ring it three times every few minutes, or if it went suddenly slack, that meant "kill the hostages."

Everyone was watching the string.

And what if he trips on something? Jeff Bob thought. What if he accidentally falls and that makes the string go slack? Then that was just too bad for the hostages.

The string tightened a bit just then, and the bell jangled, meaning everything was still going smoothly.

Some of the captive men were whispering low among themselves, and Jeff Bob didn't like that. It meant, maybe, that they were thinking about rushing the killers. And Jeff Bob had seen how trigger-happy these maniacs were. Rush them? Scratch your head too quickly and they'd probably shoot you down.

The crazies were getting edgy, too.

The young one, Johnny, was nervously humming and tapping his foot, every so often half-mumbling some heavy-metal song lyric. Ortega would glare at him when his voice got too loud.

The big room was echoey, and chilly and damp. The chairs creaked, and the old ladies whimpered. Marleen stared into space, maybe seeing her father under that mower.

Jeff Bob was trying to think of a plan.

And he looked again at the string.

Sullivan was on the roof of what had been the harware store across the street from the front of Town Hall.

He was lying flat on his belly on the black tar roof, his arms resting on his elbows, the field glasses cupping his eyes. The hardware store had a false front, pseudo-Western-style—though you couldn't get much farther east in the USA—and he was looking out a hole in it that was part of its ornate design.

He could see Swenson clearly in the bell tower.

Swenson was doing what Sullivan called "brain masturbation"—that is, he was taking drugs. Brain masturbation, of course, is different from ordinary masturbation, which does no physical harm. Brain masturbation causes brain damage.

He was snorting from two vials. One cocaine, maybe; the other . . . What? Angel dust? Speed? Most likely it was a mixture of both.

So Swenson was getting all worked up again.

"Hey, pigs!" he screamed, his voice hoarser now. "Listen, pigs—I know what you're thinking! You're thinking about waiting till dark! Maybe bluffing me till then so you can send some men in where I can't see them! Well, I got news for you—at sunset, we start executing prisoners! So if I don't get my money and some kind of guarantee by then, you're gonna lose a lot of cute old grandmothers around here!" He cackled at that.

"Just keep talking, you son of a bitch," Sullivan muttered.

He'd been thinking himself about waiting till dark. Okay, it wasn't feasible. So what was he going to do? There was one way . . .

He needed a good reliable distraction that would keep Swenson's attention glued to the side of the building where most of the visible police were clustered. Swenson made a great show of turning every minute or so to check out the broad park-lawns around the meeting hall. He had a clear view all the way around. And he knew there were cops, seen and unseen, on all sides.

If Sullivan could think of a way to keep Swenson's attention on the east side of the building for a full two minutes, the time Sullivan would have to allow to get across the street, through the parked cars and debris, across the lawn and under cover, it might be possible to—

Sullivan's strategizing was interrupted by another explosion.

Swenson had thrown a stick of TNT at a car parked on the west side. He'd glimpsed the two men hiding in it, waiting for their chance. The TNT had exploded a few feet short of the car.

"Run!" Sullivan urged, though the men couldn't hear him.

Swenson tossed another stick. The TNT turned end over end and fell lazily onto the trunk of the car. The men tried to get out—and then they were engulfed in a ball of flame as the gas tank exploded. One of them ran screaming from the wreckage, his clothing afire, the flames whipping with lashes of pain across the lawn.

Swenson lobbed another single-stick and it struck at the man's feet, exploding instantly. The SWAT operative blew into four parts, head going one way, arms, legs, and entrails another—a splash where a man had been.

Swenson howled with delight.

"You see!" he shrieked. "I'm not human! I'm superhuman! I am God on earth who sends down his thunderbolts to destroy the infidels! Follow me, drop your weapons and worship me, and I might spare you! It's no accident this was a church once! It's a sign from on high! And Jesus fucking Christ am I ever *high!*"

"Your goddamn mind has diarrhea, you asshole," Sullivan said between gritted teeth.

Damn but he wanted to squash that fly!

"I knew those bastards were down there!" Swenson shrieked. "I knew because I know *all!* Don't try to pull any more of that shit! And . . . *What?*" He pointed. "What the fuck is *that?*"

Two National Guard helicopters were approaching, fifty feet above the highest rooftop in Lightning Corners.

"Oh, hell," Sullivan murmured. He reached for the walkie-talkie Holstead had given him and depressed the call button. "Holstead? You there?"

A crackle, and then: "Read you, Specialist."

"Can you get in touch with those copters? Get 'em out of here or he'll start shooting people down there! They're blowing it for me!"

"We'll try to raise 'em," Holstead agreed.

"Get those fucking pig-fucking eggbeaters out of here," Swenson shouted, "or I'll give the kill order!"

The choppers slowed, approaching the meeting hall, and hovered low enough to make a small windstorm on the hardware-store rooftop, whipping the edge of Sullivan's coat and stinging his eyes with dust.

He waved frantically at them to get back, get back!

An impassive face with dark glasses looked down at him, and then looked up at the bell tower. They began to move in. . . .

"I'm warning you!" Swenson's voice was barely audible over the thumping of the copter blades. "Get 'em out of here!"

He raised his arm for all to see.

"See this string?" Swenson shouted. "If I go, that string signals my people downstairs!"

Sullivan could see one of the men in the copters talking on the radio now, and then conferring with the pilot. The chopper swung around and beat its way back toward the edge of town; its counterpart followed.

Sullivan blew out his cheeks. Whew.

Swenson was leaning against the bell again, his mouth lolling, his eyes turned inward to some vision.

Maybe, Sullivan thought, now was the time. . . .

But Swenson was standing straight again, checking out the lawns.

Sullivan heard a scrabbling sound behind him and looked over his shoulder. It was Beth, and someone else—a fresh-faced blond guy, couldn't have been more than twenty-one, wearing blue-tinted glasses and a SWAT getup, complete with billed blue cap. They were running in a crouch across the rooftop to Sullivan's position.

He grinned at Sullivan and squatted down beside him. Beth sat on the other side.

Sullivan sat up and stretched, asking, "Who the hell are you?" It had been a long night, and a long day, and Sullivan was in a gritty mood.

The grin melted from the boy's face. "My name's Clarke. Wally Clarke. Sharpshooter. Holstead sent me up."

"Where's the shooter you're sharp with?"

"Don't know which one to use till I talk to you, figure out ballistics, trajectory—depends on your tactics. Say, are you really the—?"

"Shut up. Now I'm thinking about finding a distraction for Quasimodo up there. Maybe a negotiator on one side who'll hold down his attention for two, maybe three minutes. That'll give me time to get to the basement windows. I spring the windows and slip

inside. One minute later you'll hear shooting. That'll
be your cue to take out the little prick in the tower."

Clarke frowned. "Yeah, but ... the loonies downstairs can see through the windows. They'll see you
coming."

Beth shook her head. "No, I spent a lot of a misera-
ble hours in that place. You can't see out the windows
very well from the floor level in there. They're set too
high. You can see out a little from the stage. But if
someone's up there, they'll still only be able to see the
front part of the lawn. He could come from the side."

Sullivan looked at Beth in admiration. All in all,
one hell of a woman.

"But what about when you come out of the basement?" Clarke demanded. "They'll see you open the
door, or hear it. These people are crazy—"

"I'll get it open quick."

"Yeah, but—"

Sullivan was losing patience. "What's the 'Yeah but'
now, kid?"

Clarke frowned. He didn't like being called "kid."
"It's just that ... Look, I know you're a good shot. I
read that thing in SOF. But nobody's that good. Those
three targets'll be spread out over the place, probably.
You'll have to swivel and fire three times, and be
accurate every time. They might have people up for
shields."

Sullivan shook his head. "No human shields. We
checked that out through the window with long-
distance scopes. They got bored with it. The kids are
sitting near the woman, but they're low. And as for
the shooting ... I don't give a rat's-ass wedding ring if
you believe I can do it or not."

"He'll do it," Beth said. "He ..." She paused. "I
know it."

But there was doubt in her voice.

Sullivan reached for the walkie-talkie.

He couldn't allow himself to have doubts.

18

When Three Minutes Take Forever

"This angle's a little difficult," Clarke admitted. "But I can hit him all right."

He had the Army Sniper Special assembled beside him.

There was something about the dubious way that Clarke was looking at the weapon that made Sullivan nervous. "Look, Clarke, that's not a Daisy Air Rifle. You sure you can use it right? You been checked out on that weapon?"

"Huh? Sure I can use it right! I haven't got a lot of experience on this baby.

"But not at this range and angle."

Sullivan looked at his watch. Where was the negotiator? It was nearly sunset. It was time to move.

Sullivan warned himself against impatience. An effective kill technician had to be prepared to work under any conditions, including the toughest of all for a man of action: delays and boredom. Add to that: fatigue. He'd been stationed here for hours, while the fatigue of a night without sleep, a firefight, and a high-stress day was beginning to congeal its poisons in his limbs, making him feel stiff and weary.

He stood up on the rooftop, still hidden from Swenson, and began to pace back and forth, stretching, grimacing at the pain in his limbs, doing knee-bends and push-ups, getting back into tone.

For a long time Swenson had been leaning against the bell in the tower, mumbling to himself. But now and then he checked the lawns, watched for the approach of the enemy. He'd seem to be sagging, falling asleep—but then the slightest movement of the police operatives along the barricade would have him up and howling.

He reacted like that now, as a black limousine drove up at the barricade. Two uniformed cops got out, and one of them opened the back door for a man in a three-piece dark suit. He was a tall, gray, fatherly man with wire-rim glasses and a briefcase. He spoke a few orders to the uniformed police, and they scrambled to obey him.

Swenson stared at him, panting.

Swenson was too far away for Sullivan to be sure he was taken in by the trick.

The negotiator was an actor, masquerading as someone High in the Government, a man of Great Power; the limousine, the police service, the conservative suit, the briefcase—all of it made him seem inordinately important. Sullivan hoped.

Anyway, Swenson was stoned. People who are stoned fixate on impressions, superficial appearances, and see more in them than is really there.

Swenson stared silently as the Negotiator stepped through the line of cops and National Guardsmen and walked up to the police barrier. Someone scuttled up and fitted him with a bullet-proof vest, which looked absurd with his suit but which gave the impression he was something precious, someone worthy of protection.

The Negotiator made an imperious gesture, an exaggeration of the arrogance of a man in power, and a cop ran up with a bullhorn.

The Negotiator put the bullhorn to his lips.

"Mr. Swenson!" his voice rang out, electronically amplified. "Can you understand me?"

"I understand you!" Swenson shouted. "Who the fuck are you?"

Sullivan was moving. He heard the Negotiator's reply as he crossed the roof to the ladder. He paused there and gave the thumbs-up signal to Clarke, then climbed down.

Beth was waiting in the alley at the bottom of the ladder.

The Negotiator's voice echoed over the rooftops. "I cannot reveal my name! Suffice it to say I'm an official of the United States government, and I'm empowered to give you what you ask for—*if* I feel it is the best course!"

"What do you mean, 'if you feel'? You want us to kill these people, pig? Because we're not playing games!"

In the alley, Sullivan was shaking his head at Beth. "Can't do it, Beth. Look if I let you come in, I risk the lives of all those people in there. I know you're competent, but everyone has something he's especially trained for. That sniper is trained for sharpshooting. I'm trained for commando work—fast work, at close quarters. You're trained in hand-to-hand—but not in this kind of shooting. Look, I'm not even letting any of the SWAT team go with me, and those guys have trained for *years*."

"Can't I even back you up?"

"I can't have that on my mind, Beth. I need as few variables as possible. That's why I won't let the police come in with me. One of them might fuck up. And I won't."

She smiled. "You arrogant bastard."

He shrugged. "It's what I'm good at."

He kissed her briefly, and walked past her.

Swenson was fuming. "What do you mean, let 'em go first? How stupid do you think I am?"

Sullivan was moving into position, to the northwest of the building. A cop, waiting crouched behind a car, handed him the crossbow with a single bolt in it. Sullivan had decided to use the .357 for the gun work.

Sullivan looked across the lawn to the small dark figure of Holstead, waiting for the signal. When Holstead judged that Swenson was completely engrossed, he'd put on his helmet.

Sullivan waited, calm, feeling the adrenaline beginning to come, focusing his mind on the job that had to be done, not permitting himself doubt or anxiety.

Once more, the Specialist was coming alive, taking over Jack Sullivan, turning him into a killing machine.

Jeff Bob didn't like the nervous way that Johnny Jensen was strutting back and forth, his fingers tightening and loosening and tightening again on his gun.

Ortega kept muttering to himself, and Esmeralda was staring at the crowd, shaking her head. "Such loathsome pigs," she was saying. "They should die *now*."

Johnny Jensen turned an imbecilic grin on her. "Yeah! Anyway, we should start killing 'em, one by one, toss 'em outside—till we get what we want!"

Completely contradicting herself, the twisted Esmeralda said, "No! We can't touch them unless Swenson says so—or if someone tries to rescue them. Or . . ." She turned to glare at the crowd. "If one of them tries to escape."

Jeff Bob tried to hear what the man with the bullhorn was saying outside, but it came all muffled and distorted through the windows.

Moving very slowly, Jeff Bob stood up, stretching his legs, which had nearly gone to sleep in the hours of sitting on the two-foot stage. He stood on the stage, doing slow knee-bends, shrugging apologetically at Esmeralda. She snorted and looked back at the frightened, fear-muted crowd in the rows of folding chairs.

Jeff Bob stood straight as he could, stretching.

Ortega was going to the window that looked out on the west lawn, deciding to take a look. Just pointless nervousness.

But then, standing on tiptoes, Jeff Bob made out the figure of a man through those windows.

Someone with a crossbow in his hand was sprinting across the lawn toward the meeting hall.

Oh shit, Jeff Bob thought. This is it.

But then he realized Ortega was about to see the guy on the lawn. . . .

Jeff Bob cried out, grabbing his right knee. 'Oh, shit . . . oh, shit, it hurts!"

He fell down, making a lot of noise, and stole a look at Ortega. It had worked. Ortega had started toward him, scowling, distracted from looking out the window.

"Fucking shut up, kid!" Ortega shouted, hitting Jeff Bob backhand so he yelped.

It hurt, but it was worth it.

Sullivan had reached the basement window, was prying it open with the knife from his boot sheath. The damn lock was old, but it didn't want to snap. Sullivan was reluctant to break the windowglass—the noise might alert the loonies.

He ground his teeth, exerting enough pressure so that either the knife or the lock had to break. The lock broke, with a *ka-chunk* sound, and he pressed the little window upward.

Then he heard something that worried him. The sound of an approaching chopper.

The choppers must have gotten word someone was trying a strike against the loonies. They'd decided to come in to give aerial backup. Or some jerk had ordered them to do that. "Shit!" Sullivan hissed. He had to move fast.

He slid feetfirst through the basement window and lowered himself to the concrete floor of the twilight-dim room. There was a broken-down Ping-Pong table to one side, and more folding chairs, folded and stacked against the wall. And there were the stairs that led upward.

The stairs would come out onto the stage, on the opposite side of the platform from those that led to the bell tower. He would be coming out behind Esmeralda, unless she'd moved.

The stairs were wooden. They would squeak. He minimized the squeaking by stepping on the place where each step had been nailed to the support. He climbed them quickly but cautiously. One small mistake now . . .

He reached the closed door at the top of the stairs—and realized it might be locked. If it were, the noise of breaking through it would give the loonies time to gather hostages for shields or to kill some of them.

Still, opening the door normally would make some noise—it looked old and creaky. So the best thing to do was to get it open fast, regardless of noise.

He stepped back, drew the Colt and looked at the door in the dim light filtering up from the windows below. He focused his mind on the place where the latch held it shut, and . . .

"I warned you about those fucking helicopters!" Swenson screamed. "And I ain't buying this negotiator bullshit! It's a trick!" He jerked the string from his wrist and let it go slack.

In the room below, the eighty-five people in their metal chairs gasped, seeing the string go slack, the bell on it fall clanging to the floor. Esmeralda laughed and turned to face them, raising the submachine gun, getting ready to blast randomly into the frightened crowd.

Jeff Bob shouted, "Marleen! Come on!" and jumped Esmeralda, grabbing the SMG and shoving it upward so it spurted its bullets harmlessly at the ceiling. Johnny and Ortega advanced toward the hostages, raising their guns. . . .

. . . Sullivan kicked hard at the spot his experience and karate training told him would break out the door's lock and swing it open fastest. His *ki* force slammed into the door, and it spun open, splinters flying. He stepped through in a completion of the kicking motion, and let his reflexes take over.

His trained reflexes guided his hands; his hands knew what to do.

His left hand, holding the crossbow so it was braced against his forearm, tracked to the left and centered on Esmeralda's heart as she kicked the children away and swung her submachine gun toward him.

Sullivan's hand, acting on its own, squeezed the crossbow trigger.

A steel-tipped shaft whispered through the air and sank to the fletching in her breastbone. He'd missed her heart, as she'd moved at the last moment. But she went down shrieking, the SMG flying free.

For Sullivan she was moving in slow motion, her arms flailing slowly as she fell, as if she were falling through syrup. He was moving with superhuman speed, which made everyone seem slow to him.

His right hand, the Colt in it cocked and ready, was seeking out two other targets. He saw Jensen running toward a cluster of frightened women to get behind them. He never got close.

The Colt drew a bead on Jensen's chest and spit fire, spinning a heavy-gauge slug to drill through the brain-fired teen's thin chest. Even at this distance, twenty-five yards—they were across the room from Sullivan—the slug sank into Jensen's right pectoral, passed between two ribs, nosed through his lungs, through his heart, and ripped out his back just below his right shoulder blade.

Sullivan swung toward Ortega, who was moving in slow motion to bring his SMG to bear on the man he thought of as "the scarface." Ortega was snarling, his eyes shining with animal hatred, face contorted. Sullivan's own face, by contrast, was stony, the expression just a shade harder than that of a great pool player about to pull off a difficult shot.

Sullivan's right hand tracked to Ortega's bald head and squeezed the trigger twice in quick succession, making the big handgun buck.

Ortega's head exploded. The SMG sprayed wildly in his hands as he squeezed it in his death spasms. The shots shattered a window, letting the rosy light of the setting sun into the room. In seconds that light changed from rosy to bloodred.

Sullivan turned toward the stairs to the bell tower.

On the hardware-store roof across from Town Hall, Clarke squeezed off two shots, having just heard the gunshots from the target area. But the big rifle jumped more than he expected it would, and it hadn't felt quite right in his hands. Maybe he *should* have put more time on it.

Because he missed.

The old, rusted bell in the squared-off tower beside Swenson rang as the shots ricocheted from it, a few inches from Swenson's head. "Lying hypocritical pigs!" Swenson screamed, throwing himself flat.

Bullets from other sharpshooters began to rip into the tower, whining around him. He wormed his way down the stairs on his belly. He was safer down here, inside the roof of the meeting hall. There was a lot more wood between him and the shooters.

The firing ceased suddenly as the sharpshooters decided he was either dead or out of their reach. SWAT teams, on Holstead's order, sprinted across the lawn.

The helicopter moved in, and a police commando on a rope ladder leapt off it onto the roof and climbed into the bell tower, unstrapping his own SMG. He looked around, then moved cautiously to the stairs. He looked down—and Swenson's Uzi burst took him full in the face. The commando was dead instantly, and pitched headlong down the stairs.

The helicopter pilot, hovering directly over the roof of the bell tower, had lost sight of the commando. He moved back to get a better sight angle, and saw only the empty stairway. He hovered, waiting, reporting on his hand mike that his partner had gone in after the target.

* * *

Sullivan had heard the bell ringing from up above. He hadn't liked the sound of it.

For whom the bell tolls? For whom *had* it tolled?

"Jack!" Beth's voice. Sullivan turned, irritated, and so didn't see Esmeralda weakly reaching out to claw at her submachine gun.

Beth was running through the front door, up the aisle, the Beretta in her hand. She reached the stage, jumped up, and then realized she didn't have a good tactician's excuse for coming.

"Uh . . . is it okay, Jack?"

"I don't know. Stay back. I've got to check out the tower—"

"Mister, look out!" shouted the kid that had wrestled with Esmeralda.

Sullivan turned. Esmeralda was sitting up, grinning at him like a vampire risen from the dead, blood dripping from her lips, the crossbow "stake" jutting from her chest. If you want to kill a vampire with a wooden stake, you've got to put it through her heart.

Sullivan raised his gun—but Beth was in his line of fire.

Beth shouted wordlessly and fired the Beretta three times. Two shots missed, a third connected as Esmeralda swiveled toward Beth and squeezed off an SMG burst. Then she fell back, twitching. Beth's third bullet had cut through the Gypsy's throat, splashing blood across the platform.

Sullivan turned to look at Beth, and groaned. Esmeralda's final burst had shattered Beth's skull.

Sullivan looked away from Beth's body and roared with rage.

He hoped to God that little prick was still alive. He badly needed to punish someone for Beth's murder.

19

Demons Belong in the Ground, Not in the Sky

The chopper pilot's name was Balzic. He had a headache, and he was tired. He was fifty-five, and looking forward to retirement. He had just about decided he was too old for the job. He had a wife and two kids, and he had seen it all and was getting a little cynical.

So when the guy in his partner's clothes climbed up the rope ladder from the top of the bell tower ... when the guy turned out to be not his partner at all, but one of those homicidal loonies ...

Well, Balzic played along.

Balzic just wasn't ready for any heroics at this stage of his career. A few more years and he could retire. So when the punk pointed the gun at him as he climbed in and gestured "Go!"—Balzic nodded wearily, and went.

Because that was an ugly-looking SMG the guy was carrying.

The loony in the stolen uniform sat on the seat beside him, and held on, cackling to himself, shouting something inaudible over the chop of the blades coming through the open door.

Balzic was trying not to think about the implications of the loony wearing that uniform. It meant Corman was dead. They'd known each other a long time.

Balzic brought the copter around, and had a glimpse of a angry looking guy with a big handgun in the bell tower, shouting something. The guy wasn't shooting—probably afraid he'd hit Balzic and bring the chopper down on the people milling on the lawn below.

Balzic expected the loony to laugh in the angry looking guy's face. But he didn't.

He looked scared.

"Get us away from here!" he screamed at Balzic, closing the door.

The chopper cut through the air toward the south.

"Get me to New York City!" Swenson screamed at Balzic.

Balzic was surprised. He would've thought this guy'd want to get as far from New York as possible.

But then, that's why they call them loonies.

Swenson's decision, though, wasn't as crazy as it seemed. He doubted there was enough fuel in the copter to get them to Canada. And once there—what? He had no money, and he'd be out in the woods somewhere.

But if he could get to Manhattan, he could find McCarter. He'd heard McCarter was staying at the Plaza for a week. The Soviet spy would have to help him—Swenson had been involved in KGB business. McCarter would have no way of knowing that Martindale had died at Swenson's hands.

Maybe he could work for the KGB, after all. Maybe an assassin. Why not? They probably paid well. Maybe they'd give him a chance at the Pope.

He'd always wanted to shoot the Pope.

But . . . that scar-faced guy. What was it Martindale had called him? "The Specialist"?

Know-it-all Esmeralda had said the guy had given

up chasing them. But that was him down in the bell tower.

Esmeralda—that lying bitch! He was better off without her. Too bad about losing Ortega, though. He was useful.

Swenson couldn't get the face of his enemy in the bell tower out of his mind. The Specialist. What was it the guy was a specialist in?

Oh, yeah. *Revenge*.

Swenson shivered.

"Get me a fucking chopper, Holstead," Sullivan said grimly.

Holstead sighed. "I don't know, Sullivan. You did a great job—wasn't your fault the bat in the belfry got away. My sergeant picked the wrong sharpshooter, that's all. And the girl, your friend—that was her fault, running in there before you were through mopping up." He cleared his throat. "I know how you feel about that. I'm sorry. But it's bad enough I let you go in—you, a wanted man, a mercenary—somebody outside the force. But to give you a . . ." He broke off, seeing Sullivan's expression.

He took a good long look at that expression. He felt a chill.

He said, "Okay. They may fry my ass for it. But okay. I'll have to go along, though. Officially, you're not here."

"Let's do it. He's getting away."

They walked across the lawn toward the line of police cars. The lawn was pocked with blast craters, still smoking, smelling of cordite. The fires in the hulks of blown cars had been put out, but the cars were blackened wrecks, like smashed beetles.

"I can't believe it," Sullivan said between clenched teeth. "The son of a bitch got away again."

"Bad luck that copter coming so near him . . . and his getting hold of that outfit. I mean, he only put on the shirt, the vest, and the hat, and we shoulda seen it wasn't our man climbing up on the copter, but . . .

Well, it seemed so crazy. Nobody . . ." Holstead's voice trailed off. "I should've gone into real estate."

Sullivan said nothing. He was trying not to think about Beth.

A TV cameraman, only just arrived on the scene— the cordon at the highway had kept them out till now—ran up to Sullivan and thrust a lens at him, as a reporter beside him, beaming, shoved a mike at Sullivan's face. "Can you give us your name, sir, and tell us—"

Sullivan lost his temper. It was all a zoo, a goddamn zoo, and that girl was dead when she shouldn't be. Someone should've stopped her from coming into the action.

Sullivan should have stopped her.

He should have found a way to protect her. He should have been faster. He should have . . .

Some part of his mind knew he was wrong to blame himself. But something else in him kept hammering it at him: It's your fault she's dead, you blew it, you should have . . . should have . . .

That was the second one he'd lost, the second girl killed because she'd been close to him.

"Should have, should have!" he shouted, taking his fury out on the annoying TV camera.

He made the index finger and middle finger of his right hand into a karate-stab ramrod and drove it into the lens, smashing the glass completely.

He withdrew his bleeding fingers and tore the camera away from the cameraman, smashed it on the sidewalk, again and again, till it was useless junk.

Then he grabbed the mike from the startled reporter and shoved it down his throat, using its cord to tie it in place. After that he spun the guy around and kicked him in the ass, so he went flying over a police barricade and onto the grass.

Not one of the cops objected to this.

"You know," Holstead said, "I always wanted to do that myself."

He went to call for another chopper.

Neither the cameraman nor the reporter was hurt badly. Later they tried to find the "unknown policeman" who'd attacked them.

But the department insisted that the guy never existed. They didn't have any cops who looked like that.

Must have been some nut, they said, who'd strayed onto the scene. You just never know.

Holstead treasured the memory for the rest of his life.

The chopper thrummed south, along the route that Swenson had apparently taken—though it was possible he'd changed course once he was out of sight of Lightning Corners.

But Sullivan thought he could guess where Swenson was headed.

New York? Then it must be McCarter. Knickian had told Sullivan that McCarter would be in town, supposedly for some conference with high-ups in the National Security Council. But McCarter—the number-two man in the Defense Intelligence Agency—probably had other business in New York. KGB business.

Sullivan hoped to God he was right about Swenson's destination. That would be too good to be true: two birds with one stone. Hit Swenson and McCarter at the same time. . . .

Forcing his mind to sort through these possibilities, Sullivan sat stone-still in the rear observer's seat, behind the pilot, watching the landscape slide by through the helicopter's bubble.

Holstead was on the chopper's radio, alerting everyone who could be alerted on short notice. A chopper is a big, conspicuous thing to run away in. Swenson would be easy to spot and intercept if he kept on in the same direction, if he didn't ditch the chopper. Sullivan hoped that Swenson just might be so stoned and shaken up he'd head with paranoid monomania to what he'd consider the nearest shelter, the organization that had sprung him from the nuthouse.

But it was a big sky, and a lot of things could happen in it.

Holstead had tried to raise the hijacked copter, but Swenson wasn't permitting the pilot to answer.

He put the hand mike on its rack and turned to Sullivan, talking louder than he needed to against the noise of the blades. "I'm beginning to think I just might have to do it!"

"Stop shouting!" Sullivan shouted.

"What?"

"I said *stop shouting!*" Sullivan bellowed. Then, seeing Holstead grinning, he realized he'd been set up. Holstead had wanted him to get mad, to blow off a little more steam.

It was obvious, looking at Sullivan, he was in a dangerous mood. That could cause a lack of cool thinking and objectivity, which could mean death for the wrong people. Holstead hadn't thought all that out. It was something he did instinctively; part of his job was psychologically nursemaiding men from time to time.

Sullivan grinned and shook his head ruefully. "Okay, okay. So what the hell are you talking about—you're beginning to think you 'just might have to do it'? Do what?"

The humor drained out of Holstead's eyes. His mouth became a thin line. "I just might have to knock that chopper out of the sky," he said, barely loud enough to hear.

Sullivan stared at him. They didn't say anything for a full minute.

"Are you crazy?" Sullivan burst out. "First there's the pilot. Second, by now they're over residential territory. The debris could kill a lot of innocent bystanders, Fred. Third . . ." He hesitated.

Holstead snorted. "Now we get the real reason. What's 'third,' Jack?"

"McCarter. If I can get McCarter and Swenson together, I'll have the goods on McCarter. Why would Swenson come to him if not because of his KGB connections?"

"Who the fuck is McCarter?"

"David McCarter. DIA. Knickian gave me good reason to believe the guy is a KGB mole."

Holstead took his turn at staring in disbelief.

Sullivan shrugged. "I know how it sounds. But McCarter is the real thing: a buried agent. And if I can follow Swenson to him—if in fact that's where Swenson's going—I'll have proof."

Holstead shook his head. "That's pretty chancy. Just not in the cards, Jack. The guy is a homicidal maniac's homicidal maniac. You know what I mean? Charles Manson puts Swenson pinups on the wall of his cell and looks at them for inspiration. I mean, if he gets a chance, he's going to kill again, and some more, and some more after that. Now, we lost a lot of people back there. We can't take the chance he might—"

"Is it your rep you're worried about or your report or what?" Sullivan snapped. "You're hot to shoot him down quick because what he did back there makes you look bad. But if you do it, the guy behind all this killing gets away. McCarter."

Holstead was scowling. "I'm not gonna kick your ass out of this eggbeater, Sullivan, only because I understand you're feeling bad. You lost your girl. So you got a right to talk shitty to me. That much. But not any more, okay?"

Sullivan's gaze didn't waver. He knew that Holstead was hedging. Holstead was a good soldier, and a good cop. But when you're a boss cop, you have to think administration and politics. Holstead had to bring Swenson down quick. To risk losing him was also to risk losing his job. That sort of thing was one reason Sullivan worked free-lance—outside the law.

"Look, Holstead, no one wants that little prick dead more than me. But it's got to be done right. If those cops who got blown up had been trained right, they wouldn't have got blown up. They didn't do the thing right. I'm just asking for a chance to do it right."

"You're asking for a helluva lot today," Holstead grumbled.

"Did I come through or not? It was your dumb-fuck sharpshooter who let Swenson get away. What the hell do they call him a sharpshooter for if he misses? He told me he could use that gun when he knew damn well he wasn't qualified for that particular piece. That's ego, not professionalism. And if your men had done what they're supposed to—see to it that no one interferes with the strike, no one goes in till the signal's given—Beth would still be . . ." He grimaced and lit a Lucky Strike.

Holstead was quiet for a while. Finally, he said, "I guess you got a point. I guess the department needs shaking up. And I guess we'll do this thing your way."

Swenson was sick.

The high had bled out of the drugs, and all that was left was disorientation, nausea, and a razor-blade-slashing headache.

"Got to pull it all together," he muttered, "or I'm fucked. The Specialist. Feel him breathing down my neck. Got to think."

The drugs made it hard to think now. The gears in his head turned creakily. But at last he saw his mistake.

"Shit," he said to the pilot. "They're going to intercept us, right? They got us on radar and they're going to cut us off, right?"

Balzic shrugged.

Swenson snarled and raised the SMG, pointing it at Balzic's head.

"You wouldn't use that," Balzic pointed out. "You can't fly this thing alone. We go down, you go too. I'll get you where you want to go. I was through being a hero years ago. But don't bullshit me with that—"

He grunted and winced as Swenson slashed the gun barrel across the side of his face. It stung like the devil.

"You think I wouldn't kill you up here?" Swenson asked, laughing. He had led a cult, and he was good at showing absolute conviction when talking about the improbable. It shone out of his eyes.

Balzic swallowed hard, seeing that look.

"I'd kill you and laugh all the way down!" Swenson said. "I've got someplace I want to go, but I'd just as soon die. I lost my comrades back there."

Balzic had no way of knowing that never had Swenson been more afraid of death than at this moment. He let out a long, slow sigh, then said, "So, they're going to intercept us. What you want me to do about it? This machine isn't armed. We can't dogfight 'em. And I'd draw the line at that anyway, submachine gun or no submachine gun. So, now what, big shot?"

"Take it down as low as you can, under any radar that might be tracking us, till I think of something else," Swenson ordered.

Balzic dipped the copter lower.

Swenson scanned the horizon. The storm that had been threatening all day was finally bursting out there. Lightning licked down through gray veils of rain. It was still a mile or two off. That might provide some cover.

"Where you think we are?" Swenson asked.

"Queens," Balzic said. "Near JFK."

"Near the airport?" Swenson thought about what he knew of New York City. He'd been out there just before he'd gotten busted the last time. There was an express train that ran from the city to a parking lot a little distance from the airport. The JFK express, right into the heart of Manhattan.

He wished to God he hadn't left the money in Esmeralda's bag. That four thou would come in handy. He might have to do this the messy way, which meant using up precious ammo. He had only two clips left, and no TNT. And he didn't want to draw attention to himself just now.

Oh, the time would come again when he'd make the world sit up and take notice. Then he'd get the attention he deserved. The women, the freedom, the money. Money translated into power, and that was the hottest drug of all. The time would come.

But now he had to make like a rat scuttling into the subways.

"You know that station where the JFK express connects with the bus to the airport?" Swenson asked.

Balzic thought. "Roughly. I can find it."

"Find it, and quick."

Balzic scanned the ground, saw a freeway he knew, made some mental calculations, and nodded to himself. He swung starboard, over a marshland. They soared low over a network of canals running between mucky patches of duck grass and high yellow reeds. The copter's fan sent waves through the patches of yellow. Then they soared over a parking lot and circled a low station building. "That's it," Balzic said. "Train just pulling in."

"Okay, take it down where we'll be screened by the reeds. There's a patch of bare ground there, see it?"

Balzic took the copter to the bare patch in the reeds and hovered over it.

He glanced at Swenson. His heart was thumping, and he thought: The bastard is going to kill me when I set down.

And they were only ten feet above the ground.

Swenson was poised by the open door, looking around like a fox sticking its head from its den. He wasn't strapped in—he was just holding on. Which gave Balzic an idea.

He heaved over viciously on the stick, so the copter tilted violently to port, pitching Swenson out the open side door headfirst.

Balzic didn't waste time looking to see if Swenson had broken his neck. He took the copter up, fast.

He heard a rattling sound from beneath, and the pinging of shots richocheting from the belly of the copter. So Swenson hadn't broken his neck. Too bad.

Balzic reached for the mike and tried to call in. But one of Swenson's shots had busted out some piece of communications equipment. All he got was static.

Balzic pulled back, ascending to well out of range of

Swenson's SMG. At this range the Uzi wouldn't be much use for accuracy.

He could see Swenson slogging through the marsh, up to his knees in water and mud, toward the parking lot. Swenson was making funny slashing motions around his face with his hand—his passage through the reeds had disturbed a host of sleeping mosquitoes. Served him right. Balzic hoped they ate him alive.

But no such luck: Swenson emerged from the reeds, scrambled up a steep slope, and came out onto the asphalt of the parking lot outside the train station. He was unslinging the Uzi—he meant to use it on anybody who tried to stop him from getting on the train without a ticket. The dumb fuck must know, Balzic thought wonderingly, that the train's operator would call ahead. But maybe he figured he could cover the guy to prevent that.

Well, there was nothing Balzic could do. His radio was busted. He had a sidearm, but it wasn't loaded and he hadn't used it in years. If he went close enough to Swenson to shoot at him, Swenson could return fire effectively. Not to mention the difficulty of firing accurately from a copter with a pistol while keeping it at hover at the same time. The damn autopilot was unreliable.

Nothing for Balzic to do but head over to JFK—he was running out of fuel and had to land soon—set her down, and tell the first guy he saw to call in about Swenson.

He swung over toward JFK, went about a fifth of a mile, and swung back.

He just couldn't do it. Unless he stopped Swenson, that loony was going to blow some people away back there.

Telling himself he was a fool, Balzic reversed course and set the copter down, sloppily, as near to the train station as he could get. He was between Swenson and the train station. He could see Swenson running toward him as he loaded his sidearm. His hand shook as he double-checked to be sure the safety was off. He got out of the chopper, shouting at the curious onlookers beside the buses in front of the station. "Get away! Run! That guy—"

Swenson came running around the chopper, firing.

You're a damn fool of a man, Balzic told himself. But at least you're dying a man.

And then Swenson cut him down.

20

Down in Kill City

"What you think Swenson will do in Manhattan?" Holstead asked. "I mean, before he gets to McCarter."

"I think he'll direct the pilot to set down at some heliport in the center of town. Maybe tell them it's an emergency landing. Then he'll make for the nearest exit and cut down anybody who stops him. After that he'll probably try to conceal the Uzi in something, or maybe use it to hijack a cab to the vicinity of wherever he thinks McCarter is. It's going to be messy."

"You don't think he'll call McCarter, have him meet him somewhere?"

"I doubt he'd trust McCarter that much. He'd want to back him into a corner and make demands."

"It could go wrong a million ways, Sullivan."

"Yeah. But when you're tracking a man, you have to go by hunches and instinct and . . . what you feel the guy is going to do based on what you know about him."

Their chopper was cruising over Queens at low altitude to avoid having to readjust for a lot of air traffic out of JFK. The rainstorm was right behind

them, catching up, sweeping the reed-patched marshland below with outrider gusts of wet wind.

The copter's lights were on; the darkness was closing fast, which would make it harder to track Swenson.

"How you going to follow the guy?"

"I was figuring on triangulating his landing with
other spotters, then having them hold off while I
landed behind him, close enough so I could spot him
leaving, follow him to McCarter or wherever he's
going."

"While he cuts a swath through the civilians down
there."

"He won't do that. He may be stoned and crazy, but
he's not really stupid. He won't want to bring the heat
down on himself."

Sullivan's weariness had burned away in the flame
of rage; all that was left was a poisonous wash of
sheer irritability.

"What's that?" the pilot asked. His searchlight was
cutting across an asphalt parking lot outside a small
train station. "There's another chopper down there.
One of ours."

Sullivan craned to look. There was a small crowd
gathered around the chopper, and a body lying on the
ground beside it, its head under a coat. A police car
was just pulling up.

Sullivan looked at the train station and nodded to
himself. "That's it," he said. "He took it down there,
killed the pilot, and got aboard the train."

"Maybe he hijacked a car instead," Holstead suggested.

The pilot called down to the patrol car to get the
whole story. Sullivan wished he had a subway map.

Swenson was, for once, pleased that he hadn't had
to kill anybody.

The people at the station had run like scared rabbits,
the cop on the train had flattened on the floor, no
trouble, when he saw the submachine gun. He'd cuffed
the cop and neutralized the driver so he couldn't use

his radio. Now he was standing beside the train driver—what did they call them? engineers?—and watching the tunnel open up endlessly in front of them.

Darkness swallowing me up, he thought. Endless darkness. The tunnels of hell. The holes in my brain.

A call came over the radio, asking if there had been any trouble, saying there'd been a report of a man with a gun.

"Turned out to be a phony gun," the train driver said to the radio as Swenson whispered it into his ear. "The guy was a harmless nut with a plastic toy. He got off already and ran like hell."

They bought the story. So they hadn't yet cross-referenced with the cops who'd found the pilot's body. The karma was working for him. Obviously his followers had been killed because the World God, the Horned One, knew that it was time for a purge.

Now he would begin his work again. With McCarter.

The man who called himself McCarter was just then nervously packing a suitcase. It was perhaps too soon to be packing—he hadn't yet received permission to leave. But he was getting strange looks from the DIA personnel. First Knickian dead, then Milner, then all these KBG men turned up dead, and the police had confirmed that one of them had been seen in the hotel where Knickian had been killed. So Knickian had something on the ball after all, McCarter's DIA associates reasoned, or else the KGB wouldn't have knocked him off. And it was said Knickian had been befriended by the Specialist. The Specialist had a rep for being on the right side. So maybe, just maybe, the thinking went, Knickian's claims about McCarter weren't so farfetched. Maybe Knickian wasn't a crank after all. Maybe . . .

McCarter had realized that morning that he was being checked out. It was time to go home. To Moscow.

His real name was Kragov. Kragov was a soft, narrow-shouldered man who looked like someone's accountant uncle, with his thick spectacles and his habit of humming to himself. He seemed hardly the sort of man who could approve the sort of horror that had been effected by Martindale and Swenson. But approve it he had, and it had gone sour. The Politburo would not be happy. Still, it was better to face them than the Americans. The Americans could be very easy on defectors. But not one who'd had his fingers in the sort of things McCarter had handled. When they found out about those years of sabotage, about the Bremmer hit . . .

Bremmer was back, and talking to the authorities. He would report that he had seen Milner—a proven KGB man now—in conference with McCarter.

No, not the United States. Defection was not the way. They'd imprison him for a long, long time. He was no longer a young man. Fifty-seven now.

And though he'd failed with the Bremmer business, Moscow would forgive him—he hoped. After all those years of service, all the information they'd had from him. Surely they could not be so ungrateful as to blame him for his failure now. Could they? No. No, he would be a hero. . . .

He looked at the two open suitcases and wondered if he'd forgotten anything. He had packed several cartons of American cigarettes, bottles of American liquor, samples of American lingerie for potential lady friends. An American Walkman. And his clothes, his passport, his . . .

His *fake* passport, he reminded himself. He had to tell himself, again and again, he was no longer David McCarter. He sighed. He was going to miss America. Especially the X-rated movies.

He found himself staring at the telephone.

He was waiting for a call. The call would tell him that it was all right to board the plane for Paris. And in Paris he would contact the men who would return him to Moscow.

He might get another kind of call. A "Sorry, comrade,

you're on your own" call. Or he might get no call at all. Which could mean they intended to liquidate him.

He opened one of the cartons of cigarettes and waited for the phone to ring.

A knock came on the door, instead.

That made him leap to his feet. He had come unarmed. He didn't believe a good undercover man should carry guns. Now he regretted that habit.

He walked toward the door . . .

And then the phone rang. He stood there a moment, looking back and forth between the door and the phone. He chose the phone.

"Mr. King?" came the voice on the other end.

Kragov smiled, and found himself relaxing. "No, this is Mr. McCarter. But I know Mr. King. If you mean Larry."

"Oh, yeah, Larry. Tell him Frank called."

"Good. When will you call again?"

"Twenty minutes."

"Okay. Good-bye." He hung up, much relieved. That had been the proper sequence of password code. His trip to Paris had been approved, the contacts for Moscow had been approved, and he would have bodyguards in his room in twenty minutes.

The smile faded from his face as the insistent knocking came at the door again.

Should he wait for the bodyguards?

"Open it or I shoot through it!" came the voice on the other side.

He didn't recognize the voice, but he had a terrible feeling he knew who it was.

Play along, he told himself. Help is on the way. Twenty minutes, they said.

He opened the door and found he had to look down to see the face of the big-talking man on the other side of the threshold. He knew the man from photos. Swenson.

Swenson pushed past him into the room. Kragov closed the door behind him.

"What do you want?" Kragov asked in his best bureaucratic chilliness.

Swenson was wearing some rumpled clothing that fit him rather badly. A plaid shirt and blue jeans. Something freshly stolen, Kragov supposed. There was mud on his shoes.

He was unwrapping a package under his arm. Something wrapped in newspaper. A submachine gun.

Kragov stared at it, disbelieving his own eyes. "How dare you bring that in here! We don't operate that way! It isn't professional to display hardware!"

Swenson laughed and sat on a chair that was too big for him. He held the SMG in his lap. "I'm not letting go of this baby till I'm free and clear. He's after me."

"Who is *after* you?" asked Kragov dryly, looking at the door. Fifteen minutes more. This madman might shoot the place up. Kragov could not afford an "incident" now.

"The scar-faced guy. Martindale called him the Specialist."

Kragov thought he had heard wrong. "Who?"

"The Specialist." Swenson seemed fascinated by the patterns in the rug. "I knew when I saw him in that tower, looking up at the copter. I knew that he was just not going to give up. He's still after me. I've got to get out of the country."

Kragov shrugged. "Then you had better head for the border."

Swenson's glare came like a sudden burst of red light. "Don't even joke about it, McCarter—or whatever your name is. You're gonna get me out of this. Or I'm going to blow you to cute little pieces." Swenson seemed to realize he was talking in the wrong tone.

"Look," the psycho went on, "I could be *useful*. I'll hit anybody—for the right pay, the right backup. I'll go to training school . . ."

Kragov snorted. "As if you'd have a third of the necessary discipline! Ha! You wouldn't last a week. No, friend, you are not one of us. We cannot help you. Except . . ." He shrugged. "I will give you some money.

That much I can do." He turned to close his suitcases. "When did you last see this scar-faced man?"

"A few hours ago."

Kragov spun to face him. "What? The Specialist is that close? You must leave here quickly!"

A light rap came on the door. Kragov stared at it, petrified.

It might be *him*.

"Frank in there?" came a low voice from the other side of the door.

Kragov relaxed a little. He went to the door and opened it. Two extremely ordinary-looking men, men picked for their neutral, mediocre appearance, stood in the hall, wearing neatly pressed double-knit suits. One he knew, the one with the glasses—Korg. The other was probably Belnoff, about whom he had heard. Said to have killed more than two dozen men.

Strange that the company of such a man should be comforting.

"Come in, come in," Kragov said fussily.

Korg came in with his .45 drawn—he had heard Swenson's voice. Belnoff closed the door behind them as they entered.

There was a moment of uncertainty as the KGB killer and the psycho killer faced one another. Then both of them looked expectantly at Kragov.

"It's all right, all right," Kragov said, waving his hand to indicate they should put away their weapons.

Korg lowered his gun but didn't holster it.

Kragov closed his other suitcase. "This is Mr. Swenson," he said over his shoulder. "He was working with Polonov and the other, you recall." He turned to Korg and Belnoff suddenly. "He has told me something . . ." He spoke in English, instinctively realizing that if they spoke in Russian Swenson would grow paranoid. Or more so. "He says that the Specialist is after him."

Korg nodded. "We believe it was the Specialist who raided the safe house at Lightning Corners." He became noticeably more nervous as a thought occurred to him: "He is after him now? *Here?*"

Swenson shrugged. "I don't know how close he is. But I know he's after me. I feel him out there."

Kragov spoke to Belnoff. "The Specialist—is he the one I'm thinking of, the one who killed Ottoowa?"

Belnoff nodded. "And the Blue Man."

Kragov's eyes widened. "The Blue Man!"

"Destroyed his entire camp."

Kragov said, "We leave. *Now.*"

Korg glanced at Swenson. "In a moment." He gave Belnoff a significant look. Belnoff looked back at him and seemed to understand.

Korg strolled casually to the window—which was behind Swenson's chair. "Let me see if the street looks safe," he muttered.

Swenson frowned and started to turn to look at Korg, but Belnoff said suddenly, "Was he a big scar-faced man, the one you think is after you?"

Swenson looked at him, then nodded slowly.

That distracted the psycho long enough. Korg stepped up behind him and pressed a gun to Swenson's head. "Move very slowly, Mr. Swenson. Put the little machine gun on the floor, please."

Swenson hesitated.

Belnoff shook his head. "Don't even think it."

Swenson ground his teeth loud enough so they could all hear it. Then he set the SMG on the floor.

Kragov picked up the gun with an expression of distaste and took the clip from it. This he hid in a potted plant in the suite's bedroom. The gun he stuck behind a drainpipe, just outside the bedroom window. He noted it was beginning to rain outside. Thunder echoed through the concrete canyons. The air was heavy with the imminence of storm.

It was dark and lightning-slashed outside. He hoped the storm wouldn't dely his plane.

"You stay with Mr. Swenson for a while, Korg," said Kragov distractedly. He drew out his wallet and put a thousand dollars on the bed. "Give him this. I suppose we need not explain to him that no one will believe him—a madman, so they say—if he tries to tell them crazy stories about Soviet agents. And those imaginary Soviet agents would then find him and kill him, somehow."

"Shouldn't we—?" Belnoff began.

"No," Kragov interrupted. "Too messy. We haven't got time to do it neatly. No, let him go." He and Belnoff—Belnoff carrying the bags—went out the door.

The storm hit the hotel with a crash and a roar and a flash of light.

Sullivan felt its full fury on the Plaza's roof. The rain stung his neck, the wind threatened to pull him off his perch. But he lowered himself over the edge of the roof nonetheless, enjoying the extra challenge.

He rappeled down two stories on the rope, between rows of windows, till he reached the one he wanted. In a lightning flash he was surprised to see that the window was open. There was a submachine gun stuck behind a drainpipe, its barrel catching the flare of lightning bolts, gleaming briefly as if with an evil smile.

Sullivan slipped through the bedroom window, and in a moment he was standing—dripping on the rug inside, listening to the voices from the sitting room. He heard someone say:

"He's somewhere near. He's going to get us all. I can feel it." Swenson's voice.

"Shut up." A voice Sullivan didn't know. A slight Russian accent.

Sullivan moved toward the door, unslinging his machine pistol, a PA3-DM, 9mm, an Argentine borrowed from Holstead's private armory. He'd fitted it with a silencer.

"We can't just sit here and wait for him to execute us!" Swenson was beginning to sound hysterical. Sullivan moved toward the door to the sitting room. It was half-open. A triangle of light fell across the rug of the bedroom from the open door, coloring it yellow. Sullivan flattened against the wall beside the door. From here he could see through the door, the two men in a mirror at the other end of the room from them. Korg was standing behind Swenson, near the window. Swenson was clutching the arms of his chair as if it were an electric chair and he was waiting for the jolt.

Sullivan waited for Korg to glance at the window, distracted by a lightning flash.

The lightning flashed . . . Korg looked.

Sullivan stepped into the room, centering the PA3's swollen muzzle on Korg's forehead. Korg brought up his gun—and didn't so much as squeeze off a shot. Sullivan's gun went *phht*! and cut a neat crease between the two halves of Korg's brain. The Soviet hardman fell back, and flailing with the dying jerk of his reflexes, smashed through the window.

He didn't fall, but hung there half slashed through by window glass, his head lolling outside, beaten by rain, his legs inside limp against the wall.

All this time Swenson was saying only "Huh-uh-*uh*!" each meaningless syllable higher-pitched than the last. He shook in his seat as if someone had thrown the switch on his electric chair.

Sullivan said, "Stand up."

Swenson took a deep breath and stood up. His pupils were pinpoints. His face was dead white.

"Go to the door to the hall," Sullivan said.

Swenson went. He moved like a robot.

"Open it," Sullivan said. Swenson opened the door. Sullivan moved in close behind him. "Hey, there, fellows," he said softly.

Kragov and Belnoff were standing at the elevator, both looking impatient. They turned to stare at him.

"You're wondering why the elevator doesn't come?" Sullivan asked. "It's because my friends with the police downstairs have had that elevator shut off. It'll never come for either of you."

He raised the PA3 keeping Swenson between him and Belnoff for a shield. "And I've got the drop on you, gentlemen," said Sullivan.

Belnoff inched a hand toward his coat.

"Yes, do take the gun out," Sullivan said. "Between two fingers. And drop it on the floor. Don't fuck around."

"Do as he says, Belnoff!" said Kragov in a quavery voice.

Belnoff dropped the gun.

"Now, both of you come in here," Sullivan said, backing up a little but never taking his eyes from them.

A minute later the four of them stood in the middle of the suite's sitting room. Swenson looked like a wax dummy. He stared at the patterns on the floor.

Belnoff and Kragov stood in their overcoats just inside the closed door. They'd left the bags in the hall.

They wouldn't be needing them.

"You're him," Kragov said in a low, squeaky voice. "The Specialist."

Sullivan nodded. He was pleased to see that Kragov was scared already. That would help.

"Sit in the chair," he said, indicating the one Swenson had sat in.

Kragov started toward the chair, then stopped, gasping. He'd seen Korg hanging in the broken glass of the window.

Belnoff saw it too, and his only reaction was a muscle twitch in the cheek.

"I said sit down, comrade," Sullivan clipped.

Kragov tore his eyes from the corpse and sat.

He stared with amazement when Sullivan tossed the gun aside.

"Come on, hitman, *hit* me," Sullivan said to Belnoff.

Belnoff grinned. "You just made the last mistake of your life," he said. He ran at Sullivan, bent forward, arms outstretched.

Sullivan feinted and ducked to one side. Belnoff adjusted neatly, pivoting on his right heel, and put his weight into a massive kung-fu slice aimed at breaking Sullivan's neck.

Sullivan was simply faster.

He ducked and took advantage of Belnoff's momentary imbalance. He kicked him in the hollow of his knees, sending him over backward to the floor. Before the Soviet agent had time to recover, Sullivan leapt up, and down, jackhammering his legs downward in mid-fall, heels together, in the center of Belnoff's chest. The "commando stomp." The weight of his body combined with his double kicking power to pile-drive into Belnoff's breastbone, crushing it, and driving slivers of bone and cartilage through lungs and heart.

Sullivan leapt clear, and stepped between Kragov and the gun. " McCarter" had been making a desperate play for the fallen machine pistol. Now he sank back into the chair. As Belnoff sank into death.

Sullivan turned to Swenson, who had watched the whole thing openmouthed, his eyes empty. Something in his head had snapped, gone catatonic. Sullivan knocked him down. He picked him up, set him up like a pin—and knocked him down again. After he'd worked off some of his anger for ten minutes or so, he grabbed the drooling man by the ankles, braced himself, and swung him around, gathering centrifugal force. He swung him around three times, and on the fourth he gave a twist of his shoulders that sent Swenson's head smashing into the wall close beside where Kragov sat. Swenson's head exploded. Kragov was splashed with blood. He yelped and started up from the chair.

Sullivan let go of Swenson's body, which fell—its head flattened like an eggshell—at Kragov's feet.

Kragov was gagging, looking green.

Sullivan went to the phone and dialed the desk. "Holstead?" he said after a moment. "Send up that FBI stenographer."

He hung up, and went to Kragov, picked him up by the lapels, and dragged him to the other end of the room. He turned him around so he could see all three bodies. "See that, McCarter?"

The man who'd called himself McCarter nodded slowly.

"You know that nowhere, no way, could you escape from me. Even under protection from American police. Even in the USSR. You know that, don't you? Look at it, at all your allies. And know."

Kragov nodded again.

"So you're going to tell the FBI everything. The location of every agent you know about in the USA. All the arrangements. Everything. Because I'll know if you hold out on them or if you're lying. You know that, don't you?"

He spun Kragov around and looked into his eyes. The two men stared into each other's souls.

Kragov looked away. And, for the third time, he nodded.

The Specialist Questionnaire

Win A Free Gift! Fill out this questionnaire and mail it today. All entries must be received by June 30, 1984. A drawing will be held in the New American Library offices in New York City on July 30, 1984. 100 winners will be randomly selected and sent a gift.

1. Book title:_____

   Book #:_____

2. Using the scale below, how would you rate this book on the following features? Please write in one rating from 0-10 for each feature in the spaces provided.

POOR		NOT SO GOOD		AVERAGE			GOOD		EXCEL-LENT	
0	1	2	3	4	5	6	7	8	9	10

RATING

Overall opinion of book....................... _____
Plot/Story .... _____
Setting/Location............................ _____
Writing style .... _____
Dialogue .... _____
Suspense .... _____
Conclusion/ending.......................... _____
Character development .... _____
Hero .... _____
Scene on front cover........................ _____
Colors of front cover........................ _____
Back cover story outline...................... _____
First page excerpts......................... _____

3. How likely are you to buy another title in The Specialist series? (Circle one number on the scale below.)

DEFI-NITELY NOT BUY		PROB-ABLY NOT BUY		NOT SURE			PROB-ABLY BUY		DEFI-NITELY BUY	
0	1	2	3	4	5	6	7	8	9	10

4. Listed below are various Action Adventure lines. Rate only those you have read using the 0-10 scale below.

POOR		NOT SO GOOD		AVERAGE			GOOD		EXCEL- LENT	
0	1	2	3	4	5	6	7	8	9	10

RATING

Able Team. . . . . _____
Death Merchant . . . . _____
Destroyer. . . . . _____
Dirty Harry. . . . . _____
Mack Bolan (Executioner). . . . . _____
Penetrator . . . . _____
Phoenix Force. . . . . _____
Specialist . . . . _____
Survivalist . . . . _____
_____ . . . . _____
_____ . . . . _____

5. Where do you usually buy your books (check one or more):
( ) Bookstore   ( ) Discount Store
( ) Supermarket   ( ) Department Store
( ) Variety Store   ( ) Other:_____
( ) Dug Store

6. What are the names of two of your favorite magazines?
1) _____
2) _____

7. What is your age? _____   Sex: ( ) Male
                                          ( ) Female

8. Marital Status: Education:
( ) Single   ( ) Grammar school or less
( ) Married   ( ) Some high school
( ) Divorced   ( ) H. S. graduate
( ) Separated   ( ) 2 yrs. college
( ) Widowed   ( ) 4 yrs. college

If you would like to participate in future research projects, please complete the following:

PRINT NAME:_____

ADDRESS:_____

CITY:_____STATE_____ZIP_____

PHONE: ( )_____

Thank you. Please send to: New American Library, Action Adventure Research Dept., 1633 Broadway, New York, New York 10019.